THE HIGHLANDS TUNNEL

The Highlands Tunnel

A Story Never Told

Dara Powers Parker

The Highlands Tunnel: A Story Never Told

Copyright © 2012 by Dara Powers Parker
All rights reserved.

ISBN 978-1482069068

Printed in the United States of America

Book design by Dara Powers Parker

Cover photographs by Frédéric Duchesnay
Author photograph by Rebekah Musser Photography

First edition: December 2012

www.darapowersparker.com

For my sons
Stage, Jackson, and Liam
Wild and free … brothers
You have what it takes

And for my father
James
My literary patron and ever a boy
With adoration and an open wallet

In memory of my grandfathers
E. B. Powers and Samuel John Ailor
Veterans of World War II
I can't wait to hear their stories again

THE HIGHLANDS TUNNEL

PROLOGUE

Man, it's dark.

I don't know where I am. Is it a cave? A castle . . . or a dungeon, maybe? I can't really tell. It's all shadows. I'm running (and stumbling) along this stone corridor—a rocky passage of darkness, gravel, and these annoying sticks that keep tripping me up and stubbing my toe.

And besides the dark—the blackness of the tunnel—there is another Dark here with me. A character, I mean, whose name is Dark. It's chasing me, and although Dark is close behind, I can't get a good look at it.

There's nowhere to turn, nowhere to hide. So I must keep running.

My heart is thumping away, wild and heavy, and my feet feel out of my control. I'm scared . . . but, at the same time, thrilled! The thing is, I know this is a dream. Not that that makes the danger feel *any less real. But typically, when I'm being chased in a nightmare, I can't make my body work right. I can't escape and I can't fight. I'm helpless. Frozen. But now—look at me—I'm running!*

Despite the constant tripping, I feel powerful. I check my hands for weapons. Nothing. I just know I have what it takes to defeat it . . . whatever it is. If I can only find some advantage, some twist in the road that will allow me to surprise it. . . .

When I chance a look back I see the Dark, like a liquid sheet of black being shaken out. Darth Vader's cape. It's gaining on me, coming to capture me in its shadow.

You know, I'm just a regular guy. I help out around the house, usually finish my homework, and can't wait to drive cars. But here I am in danger . . . and I like it.
Totally afraid and totally stoked.

I think I'm coming to the exit at the end of the passage, but the Dark stacks some sort of clutter to trap me—boulders, I think. I must climb to the top and face this thing that is after me. When I reach the blockade, however, the Dark disappears—dissolves really, like the smoke of a steam engine in the wind.

I turn around now to find the way out, and I see a speck of light. I run toward it, knowing that if I can reach the light, the thing will lose its hold on me. I run and the point of brightness grows bigger and bigger, until finally—

Wait a sec!

I can see what it is that was after me. Only, the Dark in the tunnel is not chasing me. Maybe it never was. It's scrambling—trying to outrun me.

I'm chasing it!

1. THE GETAWAY

"Harrison, will you get the eggs for me?" the mother asked her son, knowing without looking his way that he would oblige. "Thank you, darling. You are so helpful."

Harrison momentarily looked beyond the counter where his mother was making a quiche. He could see the green outdoors through the warped farmhouse windows of the kitchen. His younger brother, Wheeler, was digging at the base of a tree.

He ought to point this out to their mother, he thought. She wouldn't want Wheeler mucking up the mulch beds. Feeling a surge of goodwill, however, he surreptitiously waved to his brother from the window. Then he made a slicing motion across his throat with his fingers, meaning "Cut it out!" Wheeler dismissed him with a return wave.

Thank goodness for all these tall windows, Harrison was thinking. It didn't matter how gray the day was, his father insisted that no lights be turned on until dark. The house existed on natural light until the sun was well down. Still, the old glass bothered

Harrison. He would swing his neck trying to find a view of the outdoors that wasn't wiggly. It made him think that everything outside the somber house wasn't real—like it was painted.

But then everything on the inside was colorless and shadowy. If he could just get on the other side of that glass. . . .

He started to think up reasons to leave the kitchen and go outside. Only . . . his mother needed him. He sighed, looking back to the mess of ingredients starting to crowd the work surface and resigned himself to helping with dinner.

Harrison turned on the oven to preheat. His mother swiveled around at the sound of the oven firing up.

"Oh, thank you. I forgot to do that. I can always count on you, right?" She kissed his forehead then rubbed it away on her route to the refrigerator. "Oh, no! The half-and-half. Shoot!" She slapped a hand to her head in hopelessness.

"Why not use milk?" the son asked hesitantly, hoping instead he would be sent on the errand. Could this be his ticket out?

"No," she sighed, "the recipe calls for half-and-half." Harrison brightened at his mother's compliance. "Will you ask your father to drive you to Kessler's? No, never mind. He's watching the game."

"I'll ride my bike," he offered quickly.

"Really?" Her question was unnecessary. "Let me get you some cash."

On his way out, Harrison poked his head into the room where his father was watching television while assembling miniature accessories for his model railroad. He had newspaper spread out over the wooden floorboards, and it looked like he was working on the high school football stadium—two yellow goalposts waited for installation while he glued little people onto bleachers.

The project train layout took up the whole cellar, and his father used his seldom-had free time to add to it, positioning small mossy trees or tiny park benches. Harrison had helped him install the electricity and build the plywood supports. Wheeler liked to help paint and run track.

It was an authentic scale model of Grant, their little hometown—every detail true to life, except that there was no actual railroad in Grant. Although the village in reality was small—population under a thousand—seeing it in miniature somehow enlarged it in the viewer's mind. A little world that operated by itself with the flip of a light switch.

The high school was in fact in the neighboring town, accommodating the western side of their county. Harrison realized for the first time—noting the football stadium taking shape—that his father's replica had outgrown their town and he was expanding. *Is there room in the cellar for this?* he wondered suspiciously.

"Bye, Dad. I'm going for a ride."

"Yeah? Where to?"

"Kessler's. Gotta pick up some stuff or dinner

won't happen."

"What is for dinner?" The father only glanced away from the gluing activity for a second.

"Quiche."

"Do guys eat quiche?"

Harrison shrugged. His father pulled a wallet from his back pocket and offered it to his son. "Will you get me a hot dog?"

"Sure."

Harrison knew he wanted a hot dog from the vendor outside of the hardware store. It was called the Mighty Midget Kitchen, a small metal trailer/diner parked on the sidewalk downtown. He had watched his father order a hot dog with mustard and onions from the skinny bald man countless times. That was back when Harrison would go to work with his dad, a builder. The downtown office was located on Main Street, above the bike repair shop, across from the Mighty Midget.

The problem was, Harrison's mother was never too keen to the idea of her children walking around rooftops, carrying saws, and dodging heavy machinery. She objected and finally got her way, saying that Harrison needed to study and the work was too dangerous for young Wheeler.

Harrison was fourteen and hadn't hung out with his dad since then . . . two and a half years about. Now he helped his mother make quiche.

He still felt as though he understood his dad, even if their conversations consisted of the father asking a question and the son answering it—unless, of course, the question was rhetorical, which happened a lot, and rendered Harrison speechless. Nonetheless, he liked the interaction with his father better than answering his mother's questions, which were often less genuine—born out of skepticism or politeness.

Thus, this secret hot dog mission was important. His father trusted him, not only with his wallet, but also with the details of the culinary contraband. He knew Harrison would keep it a secret. Perhaps this would become the first in a series of runs.

The son was considering this as he stomped up the stairs to his room for a jacket. He passed the old writing desk on the landing. This house had once belonged to a famous author, whose name Harrison did not remember. But he often wondered how that guy could do any writing in this dark alcove. It was hard enough to *see* in this house. There was no escaping the gloom.

Still, Harrison's father was attached to the farmhouse. He often pointed out its old-timey features and said you couldn't find—or recreate—such treasures in new homes. Besides, he maintained schemes to update the architecture in the future—when he could get the extra money and the time to make his blueprints reality.

The floor in Harrison's room slanted slightly toward the back of the house, but Harrison couldn't feel the imbalance anymore. He walked the length of his room to the window, passing his open physics book on the floor. He chose not to think about the homework he was neglecting and Mrs. Byrne's disapproving stare. Through the bubbly glass he could see Wheeler still messing around under the trees.

After grabbing a zippered cardigan, he passed his old dresser and mirror. He would often stare at his reflection in the glass, scorn his lanky form and shaggy head, and wonder when he would start to fill out. Like the windows, the mirror was antique, reflecting a cloudy and spotted image.

Not pausing to look this time, Harrison left the house and walked to the barn for his bike.

He was glad for a reason to go out. He wanted to belong to the world, not just look at it from the inside. But the thought of leaving without giving his little brother a hard time was quickly dismissed.

"Wheeler, what are you doing?" he inquired critically.

The boy looked up from the dirt. "Look what I found." It was an old chewing tobacco tin.

"Wow," Harrison replied flatly.

"I wonder who it belonged to. Maybe a cowboy—"

"Well, being that this isn't the West. . . ."

"Then an outlaw hiding out. Like Bonnie and Clyde."

"Probably a farmhand."

Wheeler dropped the tin and brushed his dirty fingers on his jeans. "Where are you going?"

Aw, man! He knew the risk of Wheeler wanting to go, but he had chosen the detour anyway. His brother was three years younger and quite a handful.

"I'm going to the store," Harrison admitted. He couldn't help bragging. "I got Dad's wallet."

"Can I go, too?"

"Only if you go tell Mom."

"Oh, she doesn't care. Wait. I'll get my bike."

THE HIGHLANDS TUNNEL

2. HAUNTED

Wheeler rode ahead of Harrison. The farm's driveway was almost a quarter mile uphill . . . in both directions. His family didn't own the land—just the house and a decent piece of yard, which contained seven enormous evergreens, whose shade was responsible for the murky indoors.

They traveled past the burro, Dudley, whose head looked two times too big for its body. Harrison always thought it was the cutest thing ever, with its long upright ears that flopped at the ends. Wheeler used to tease it, but it had earned everybody's respect recently when it killed a coyote that was after the calves. It had always been a noisy and cantankerous little beast, but no one suspected it of being lethal.

Turning onto the dirt road that led to town, the two brothers expertly swerved around a momma duck and her ducklings, which had waddled up to the road from the pond. A yellow horse hung its head over the fence, hoping for company. Wheeler flashed it a wave, but the boys flew past without stopping. In the distance, Harrison barely took notice of the blurry outline of pale blue that indicated the foothills of the nearest mountain range to the west.

His eyes skimmed over to the blinking tower lights on top of Mount Tempest. The mountain was said to shelter an underground government or evacuation location for the heads of state in case of an attack or some other national emergency. There had even been a mysterious plane crash up there years ago that people still gossiped about.

Oh, how those lights always captured Harrison's attention and jumpstarted the daydreams!

Reminiscing of local lore, he recalled his dream of the night before—the one in which something he couldn't see was chasing him. It felt curious and exhilarating. Although he obsessed over Indiana Jones movies and *The Lord of the Rings*, these days he preferred to stay out of trouble himself.

But the dream concerned him because he thought he had grown out of it.

It all started before he could remember—his craving for something more than ordinary life. When he was younger, he tried to research it by giving in to certain impulses. Wheeler and Harrison's best friend, Luke, were always too willing to help.

They would stack up boxes in their parents' walk-in closet, carefully climb up, and lift the board in the ceiling that served as the entryway to the attic. The boys would negotiate their bodies through the opening and explore the area under the rafters, searching for evidence of ghosts or things left buried in the dust that might conjure up a mystery to be solved.

There was the time he, Luke, and Wheeler designed and dug an intricate underground tunnel through the yard. It was supposed to be a secret passageway from the smokehouse to the shed. His mother would have never known had it not been for the disastrous cave-in that halted production.

On another adventure, he and some guys from school, including Luke, sneaked out and hiked up Mount Tempest in the night. Harrison was careful to keep this mission a secret, even from Wheeler. The little brother would have been too keyed up to keep quiet, and they would have been found out for sure. Besides, Harrison did not want to be responsible for Wheeler's arrest or disappearance . . . or whatever might have happened when the G-men caught them.

It was summer and they dressed all in black, following the deserted road the whole way. They found a fenced compound disguised as the Emergency Broadcasting organization that's responsible for those high-pitched "tests" on the radio and television. Harrison had expected some military police action that night, but nobody seemed to notice them. He liked to think that they were being watched, but that perhaps junior-high-school kids in black didn't pose enough of a threat to necessitate action. He had squinted his eyes in disappointment, ignoring the pale yellow sunrise that confronted him on the way home. He had made it back in bed by the time his family was waking up and his parents knew no better.

THE HIGHLANDS TUNNEL

In sixth grade, Harrison and Luke established an organization, Spirit International, which studied the paranormal. They passed out their homemade, Crayola-markered blue-and-red business cards to their class and Boy Scout troop. Kids would enlist their help with chairs that rocked themselves, Indian burial grounds, and bumps in the night. He and Luke would research the history of the area, which was often connected to Civil—or even Revolutionary—War activity. Then, with their tape recorder and notebook, they would spend the night at said haunted setting, recording data and deliciously frightened out of their wits.

When he indulged himself like this, he was in the moment—excited and scared, not too concerned with the results. He was digging the tunnel, not worrying about its completion. He was sneaking out, not anticipating lock-down at Guantanamo Bay. He didn't used to care about consequences or judgments. It was intense and inspiring.

However, he and Wheeler had really angered the grownups when they set off firecrackers in the abandoned barn and silo across the road from his house. Like a good big brother, Harrison took the blame, saying he acted alone. He's not sure now what they thought the outcome would be, but it resulted in an uncontrollable fire, community service, and a criminal record for Harrison.

"Not cool," his dad had muttered crossly under his breath.

It was at this time that Harrison decided to tone it

down for a bit. These episodes were only snacks to feed the creature; after the thrill faded and it smelled the leftovers, the monster salivated for more of a meal.

Eventually he discovered that this appetite didn't do anything for him except get him into trouble. These days he mostly stuck to his movies and books. He especially appreciated the urban legends that saturated this land around the nation's capital. Conspiracy theories and spies and all that. But besides the anticlimactic trek to Mount Tempest, he had never personally experienced any of it.

He could read about it, sure, but he just figured he wasn't made for that sort of thing.

Harrison's father's father, for whom Harrison was named, flew a bomber in the war . . . which sounds heroic, but it wasn't like that. The story goes that he was piloting a run and bailed out over Switzerland. No one saw him, the plane, or his crew ever again, so the grandfather couldn't defend himself or explain what happened. Maybe it was enemy flak or engine failure, but it sure sounded like desertion.

While he was stationed overseas, the disreputable pilot had met Harrison's grandmother, a petite French woman, who nowadays, with dyed and curled black hair and glittering blue eyes, took on the world with her walking cane. He had married her and left her in Paris with a baby on the way. The Air Force had agreed to send her and her family to the States after her husband disappeared. She didn't believe the defection story, and for several years after her immigration to Washington, D.C., she had stalked the military for more information . . . even when the officials persisted to hold to the theory that he had died after bailing out during a run. She finally gave up when all her leads came to dead ends, but she kept the folded flag on the mantel in memory of the man she had married but had hardly known.

The name bothered Harrison. He once asked his dad why they named him after his grandfather—the deserter.

"Well, because I'm named for my grandfather. Of course, it's my maternal grandfather, but you didn't want to be named Norman, did you?" He had laughed, and Harrison had scowled. He wondered what his father was thinking; you don't joke around when you name your kids. Maybe his father, like the grandmother, didn't buy the Switzerland story. Regardless of what he believed, Harrison's dad didn't talk about it, so there was no way to know.

Although Harrison used to go looking for the supernatural, this was one ghost he definitely didn't want to find.

Perhaps the grandfather had survived the jump from the plane and lived to shirk his responsibility to his young wife and unborn child. He may still be alive, giving out coins—like Luke's granddad did—to his European grandchildren. Although curiosity got the better of him and he sometimes wondered about the man's fate, Harrison wouldn't want to meet his grandfather . . . alive or not.

His friend Luke's grandfather was in the South Pacific during the war. When Luke's mother wasn't around to shush him, "Pop," as he was called, would tell the boys frightening tales with a big grin on his face. The stories included a great white shark, a Navajo Indian code talker with a peace pipe, and little island boys who would bring the American soldiers the enemies' heads in exchange for Hershey chocolate bars. From his cheery affect and benign approach, you would never guess that Pop had lived this sort of momentous youth. When not reliving the past, he spent his time hair spraying his sparse comb-over into position and lecturing the grandchildren on the necessity of using a daily hair conditioner.

Harrison told Luke that his own grandfather's plane went down and left it at that. He couldn't admit to his friend the truth that his namesake was a traitor. Listening to Pop, Harrison thought how easy that era seemed. Sure, there was a war and an enemy. It was life and death on the war front, but the boys knew what to do—knew what was right. They joined up and fought together for what was good, sometimes sacrificing their lives for that ideal. It was deadly and wretched, but at least they were esteemed for it. If they died, they could at least feel good about why. They had died heroes.

Like it was a genetic trait, Harrison supposed his grandfather didn't have the hero gene in him. Maybe he couldn't handle the fear. That seemed somewhat understandable. When Harrison tried to visualize himself sitting in the cockpit of a bomber headed toward heavy flak—probably watching fellow airmen bailing or going down in their planes—he could feel real fear conjured up by his imagination. But then he would remind himself that he lived in a safe world.

It all seemed so far away—not reality, but an adventure story for old guys with watery eyes to reminisce about.

Well, there was no war anymore. No adventure. No enemy. Nothing to fight for. At least not that Harrison could see.

3. THE CRIME

Wheeler stopped at the end of the road and waited until Harrison braked to a slow roll next to him.

Both feet back on the pedals, they turned a slight left, passing the Quaker meetinghouse on the corner. The downtown up ahead was packed tight and the road closed off to traffic. It was the annual arts and crafts festival. The sidewalks were flanked by tents, easels, and lots of people. Women wore high-heeled sandals and sundresses with wide-brimmed hats. Men in expensive sunglasses walked dogs and children on leashes.

Harrison got off his bike at the line of shops along the main street.

"What are you doing? I thought you needed groceries," Wheeler questioned. Kessler's was farther down the road, past these rows of stacked buildings.

"I got to stop at the Mighty Midget first."

"Can I get something, too?"

"It'll ruin your dinner," Harrison replied, much like a parent.

"Pleeease," Wheeler whined.

Ignoring him, Harrison stepped up to the "Order Here" window. Resembling an old silver camper—but one-third the size—the Mighty Midget Kitchen was crammed into the space between the hardware store and antique shop. The painted red lettering looked new, although the style was most definitely from another decade—an era in which everything was designed to resemble rocket ships.

"A hot dog with mustard and onions, please," he requested.

"Harry! Is that you?" asked the elderly vendor, who looked too tall to fit in the Midget Kitchen. "Haven't seen you in a good while. How's it going?"

"Good, sir." Harrison was not fond of his given name, but he absolutely hated the diminutive.

"This must be for your father. I'll make it just the way he likes it—a lot of onions and a little mustard."

"*Blech!*" Wheeler protested. "A pretzel, too, please," he added for himself.

"Coming right up, young man," said the hot dog man, lighting up a smile for Wheeler. He wore a paper hat and an apron. "Anything for you, Harry?"

"Not this time, thanks."

"You know, I've been fixing your dad's hot dogs since before you were born. When will school let out for you all?"

"Soon, sir. Next month," Harrison replied politely.

Wheeler stood on his toes and looked inside the dark capsule. Besides a cook top and some supplies, there wasn't much else to see.

Harrison rubbernecked up and down the street, surveying the artists' booths. "C'mon, Wheeler. Let's look around," he directed as other hungry customers approached the Mighty Midget. "We'll be back, sir," he told the man.

The boys leaned their bikes against the nearby brick wall and walked a ways, passing several tents exhibiting pottery, jewelry, and fabrics. Wheeler suddenly bolted down the street, calling, "Look at this, Harrison!"

It was a booth full of the brothers' favorite form of art: weaponry. Handmade knives, spears, and machetes mostly, as well as bows and arrows, carved and painted Caribbean-style, were displayed on tables and leaning against the walls of the tent.

"Righteous," Harrison whispered as he tried to penetrate the crowd of people to better view the wares. The vendor, who Harrison supposed was also the artist, was haggling with a customer in a loud exaggerated accent. His hair was wild, his eyes—although lightly colored—full of shadows, and his manner was slightly out of control.

When some of the crowd emptied out, Harrison found himself standing next to Maggie Rios, a girl from school.

"Hi, Harry!" she said enthusiastically.

"Hey, Maggie. It's Harri-son, actually. I dropped the Harry like two years ago."

"But Harry's a fine name—a good guy's name," she argued.

"I'm not a good guy," he said. "I'm Harrison."

"Oh, I know that," she declared non-defensively. "I just thought that maybe you're like me and prefer a nickname." She was looking at the table again, but she continued to chatter. "My real name is Margarita Elana Castillo-Rios. It's way too grand, I know. So I go by Maggie, even though we once had a little dog named Maggie. I don't care. My dad still calls me Margarita, though."

Harrison smiled and sniffed. He hadn't seen Maggie for a while. She was one year behind him in school, so she was still at the junior high.

When she reached out to touch an item on the display, her sweater brushed his arm. It was thick but as coarse as rope and the same color, too. He noticed her skirt, on the other hand, which was quite stylish. Her hair was long and black with lighter brown streaks in it. Had his eyes stayed there, he may have compared it to streams of butter running across a dark slice of pumpernickel bread. Instead, he was thinking about picking up the hot dog.

In their little village of Grant, there were two roads that forked into the main street, which led to the downtown area. On one of those forks lived the landowners; on the other lived the people that worked the land . . . or cleaned the others' homes. Maggie lived on that latter road, and Harrison lived on the former.

"My father is from a family of aristocrats, but he became a famous boxer. He won a lot of fight money for himself, even though he didn't need it. He was born with a trust."

Maggie was always telling these ridiculous stories about her family in Mexico.

"His mother, my *abuelita*, gave me this skirt. See?" she asked, giving a little twirl so Harrison could see the rainbow of colors underneath the sheer-black top layer. She was still touching the knife on the display table. The wooden handle was painted and it came with a fringed leather sheath and a high price tag.

Her father, Diego Castillo, had started working for Harrison's dad a few years back. When she was younger, Maggie had spent the afternoons after school at the Bentleys' home. What Harrison recalled most about her visits was that she would eat all their food.

Maggie continued to prattle, but when she paused for a moment, Harrison quickly got in, "I'm named after my grandfather. He was in the war."

"Cool," she replied.

It was then that the vendor charged up behind them. He leaned aggressively between Harrison and Maggie and stared at an empty space on the table. His wide eyes matched the color of his tanned skin. Harrison, following the man's gaze, was surprised to see the knife that Maggie was touching had disappeared.

"It's gone," the man exclaimed in his thunderous island inflection. His eyes automatically darted from Harrison to Maggie, then down to the front pocket of her hooded sweater. "Let me see what's in your pocket there, girl!"

Maggie's mouth fell open and she looked like she

would faint. Her hands dropped protectively to cover the pocket. "Nothing," she practically screamed at his accusation.

The man took a few long steps to the entrance of the tent and hollered, "Hey! I need police—I've got a thief here!" His gold eyes gleamed, fierce and active. "You stay here, girl," he ordered.

"Harrison, you were standing next to me. Tell him I didn't take it!" Maggie pleaded.

He wanted to, really, but he wasn't sure that she hadn't. At his hesitation, her face fell.

"Please, tell him." Her lower lip started to tremble. Harrison glanced from Maggie's face to the tent exit. He understood that such a crime in their little town could mean big trouble for her family.

And all of a sudden, as though time stood still, he was aware that something was watching this, waiting for his reaction. A presence—not physical, but substantial nonetheless—an invisible audience tracking this scene as it played out. What it was, he couldn't say. Good or bad, he didn't know. But he had someone's—or something's—attention. And he knew that his choice would affect the rest of his existence.

Looking back into Maggie's eyes in that moment, this cautious boy chose impulsively to believe her.

4. RUNNING

"What's up, Harrison?" Wheeler asked warily, crossing from the other side of the booth.

What *was* up? What should he do? The few Jamaicans Harrison had met were all groovy—"No worries, mon!"—but this strange Caribbean fellow operated like a loose cannon, and he wasn't too keen on the idea of standing up to him. Avoid all confrontation was his usual tactic—slip under the radar. If he could get Maggie away from the scene of the crime, they could fetch her father to help diffuse the situation.

With only a second left to determine a course of action, he decided that they would make a run for it. He thought self-righteously that this was out of character for him, but he didn't yet know himself very well.

Harrison grabbed Maggie's arm in one hand and Wheeler's jacket collar in the other. "Let's go," he commanded, quickly and confidently slipping out and releasing them into the crowd, just as an officer reached the irate craftsman.

They heard the man yell after them, and so they appropriately picked up the pace, dodging products and pedestrians. The art show was a haze of colors as they sprinted and weaved.

Harrison thought about how less than an hour ago he had been a responsible son making quiche, trusted with his mother's grocery errand and his father's wallet and hot dog request. Now he was running from the police with his little brother and a suspected felon. Could he be charged with aiding and abetting a criminal?

The entire town must have figured out by then what was going on—three kids running through the street being chased by law enforcement made it pretty obvious. Harrison could see the suspect in the people's expressions, and yet nobody tried to stop them. Fortunately most of the patrons were out-of-towners. He only hoped they wouldn't be noticed by anyone who knew their parents.

He couldn't help but remember running from that dark thing in his dream. In reality, though, being chased by a cop and an angry Jamaican was not as fun. The adrenaline made him feel sick and his head spun.

Unfortunately, while trying to avoid several small children in strollers, Harrison stumbled into a shelf holding painted pottery, which crashed onto the pavement. There were some impressive gasps from the onlookers, and that's when he looked right into the face of their neighbor Mrs. Dunbar, who gave him an astonished stare. She would no doubt remember the barn fire of two years ago and catalogue both incidents in the same file—the one that read, "Harrison Bentley's

Criminal Youth." After a brief hesitation, the three kept moving.

With heavy breaths, Wheeler managed to pant, "The Mighty . . . Midget." Harrison glared at his brother in disbelief, assuming he wanted his food order. But then Wheeler added, "He'll help us."

Harrison knew he was right. Although they didn't even know the man's name, the hot dog man was a friend. If he made them turn themselves in, at least he would be there to help with their defense. Furthermore, the kitchen was the gateway to the only alley between the downtown shops. That alley provided the exclusive escape from Main Street.

When they reached the silver capsule, their feet pounding the brick sidewalk, the hot dog man jutted his long neck out the window. "What's wrong, kids?"

"They think she stole something!" Harrison, out of breath, gestured to Maggie.

"Over here," the man pointed to the left of the little shelter. The kids hurried to its side as the old guy opened a small door. He looked concerned rather than judgmental, and for that Harrison was relieved.

Stepping in, he was amazed to find a largeness inside the little kitchen, as though it were a dark cavern. Then the man, leading them to a line of steel cabinets, told them to sit on the floor.

"Try to stay down until I can see that it's calm," he said.

Harrison tried to focus on the interior of the Mighty Midget, but he couldn't see much. He listened nervously to Maggie, who was trying to cry quietly. He remembered that she could be quite emotional.

"How long will we have to hide?" Wheeler whispered.

"I don't know. I hope not long. Mom doesn't even know you're with me."

At this Maggie sobbed.

Peering over Harrison's knees, Wheeler said comically, "Oh hi, Maggie. How's it going?" After throwing him a stern glower, she began to giggle through her tears.

It was clear from his expression that Wheeler was somewhat enjoying himself.

"My feet hurt," Maggie complained as she ran a finger around the inside of her leather flat.

Her tears stirred up a strange sensation in Harrison. He felt annoyed but, at the same time, protective of her.

He was gasping and wheezing. In the metal hollowness of their hideaway, his breathing echoed.

Last November, during a basketball game, he had taken a hit to the nose. The bones had crushed his sinuses, and he couldn't breathe through his nostrils. Since the accident, the challenge was always to get enough air into his lungs when running (another difference he didn't encounter in his dream).

He wished he could say that the injury came from hitting the floor after a nasty foul or sacrificially taking an elbow to the face. Instead, he had been watching Tabitha, a pretty tenth-grade girl in the bleachers, and while he wasn't paying attention, a teammate forcibly passed him the ball, which broke his nose on impact. Not his best moment.

A low gravelly whine interrupted his memories and followed with a jab of soft, wet pressure. A white face with one obscured eye emerged from the darkness. It was an enormous dog—a Great Dane, white with dark-gray patches.

"You have a dog in here," Harrison whispered urgently.

"Yes," the old man answered, as if nothing were unusual about a gigantic dog in the Mighty Midget Kitchen.

He reached overhead and pulled a metal slatted screen down to cover the access window and turned around. He hung a towel on his shoulder and adjusted the white paper hat, which was shaped like an army garrison cap.

"I'm afraid you three have created quite a stir out there."

"What should we do?" Harrison asked. The dog was taking turns licking Wheeler and Maggie on their faces.

"Well, I don't think you can stay here. I'm not suited to defend you. I only keep the doors open."

Harrison thought that was an odd comment to make, but he let it go, figuring that the diner's profits made up the man's living and he would certainly want to stay operable during the bustling fair. The old cook started pulling out edible items from the overhead shelves. "But I'm going to fix you something to eat, and then I can help you escape."

"Oh, man! Mom is going to be so ticked," Wheeler blurted out.

The hot dog man moved about the space as he worked. "What do you think of the place?"

"It's bigger than it looks," Harrison replied, grateful for a distraction. "Where did it come from?"

"After the war, I used to man this kitchen in the city. It was inside the belly of Union Station." He was referring to the big train hub in Washington, D.C., which was thirty or so miles away. "I fixed subs and hot dogs for all the returning soldiers and travelers on their way to the gates. A lot of passengers boarded their trains with meals from this stove. After so many decades of the rush, I decided to move out to the country."

Maggie, Harrison, and Wheeler thought they could hear the underground, yawning echo of train whistles and passengers headed to the tracks.

The dog helped pull them out of their panic as they rubbed its velvety fur. Harrison could feel its steady heartbeat as he kneaded the loose skin on the dog's chest. Its tail rhythmically slapped the man's legs as he worked.

"Isn't he a fine dog?" he asked with a proud smile. "The health department's never found us out.... Isn't that right, boy?"

The Great Dane looked up at him, and his owner tossed it a hot dog, which it caught with barely a motion.

"Okay. You'll have to go out the alley way," the man continued. He was wrapping food into small foil packages. "Here you go. These will fit in your pocket, there," he pointed to Maggie's sweater pouch, and she stuffed them inside.

"Actually, sir," Harrison started, "my mom's making quiche."

"Oh, you can't go home," the man declared, throwing him an *are-you-out-of-your-mind?* glare. "You've been running from law enforcement. You can't stop now. This young lady is wanted for shoplifting, and you just shattered hundreds of dollars worth of merchandise. Besides, Helen Dunbar saw the whole thing."

How did he know all that?

"It's all just a mistake!" Harrison exclaimed.

But reviewing the man's synopsis of their situation, he felt trapped and angry. He frowned at Maggie. For all he knew that knife might be hidden in her sweater with the Mighty Midget take-out. Maggie seemed to know what he was thinking and looked hurt.

"Let's go," said the man. "You've got a train to catch."

"What?" Harrison shouted, in shock. He couldn't believe what he had just heard. A sarcastic laugh-half-snort came from him. "We're just kids—not tramps!"

"Don't worry, Harry. You don't need a ticket. But you will have to be smart. Stay hidden as long as you can."

Wheeler moaned. "Wait. The train station is like

a hundred miles from here. There aren't even train tracks in Grant." He was quite ready to jump a train but couldn't comprehend it. The train station was in fact eleven miles east, but it would take several hours to walk to it, and it was already evening.

"We're not taking a train anywhere," said Harrison firmly.

At that point a severe knocking on the window screen shook the diner.

The old man startled at the noise but did not look surprised. He insisted in a hushed hurry, "Of course you are. The train station is actually quite near. But you will need to go straight there and board the coaches. Here's the back door. Be careful." He thrust a hand out to Harrison. "By the way, I'm a Harry, too. I'm Harold."

Harrison was convinced that the old guy was crazy. *He thinks he's still at Union Station.* But he was definitely not going to head out the front to see who was knocking.

"Thanks for your help, sir," he said quietly, shaking his hand. The banging started up again and the dog whined, its clicking toenails making anxious music on the metal floor.

"You take care of Maggie and Wheeler. I'll take care of the bikes, and the dog will show you the way," Harold said as he held the door for them. Harrison, Wheeler, Maggie, and the big dog exited the vessel. The four bandits heard the door thud behind them, and that was that.

Before them stretched the long alley between the hardware and antique shops. The dog woofed awkwardly and trotted off between the two brick walls, which incidentally reminded Harrison of a labyrinth with no turns.

It was dark—not only because of the tall buildings blocking the light, but because the sky had changed to a smoky blue. They couldn't see beyond the lane. It was all shadows, and the spotted white dog turned to gray and disappeared into the gloom.

THE HIGHLANDS TUNNEL

5. THE DEPOT

The three stragglers moved through the alleyway, swift but stealthy, looking back habitually as if they were being followed. When they had walked the length of the buildings, they crossed a back road comprised of uneven cobblestone, gravel dust, and weeds. None took notice of the conflicting stillness that should have been the distant babble of the art fair. In the dusk, straight ahead, Harrison glimpsed an unfamiliar construction on which the dog stood.

Wheeler looked at Maggie and his brother. "I've never seen this place before." The boys had lived in Grant their whole lives and knew all its attractions. Wheeler ran up the stone steps, in between the wooden benches, past the wrought-iron banister to the edge of the platform. He stared down about a foot to find—remarkably—a single line of train tracks.

Harrison and Maggie and the dog followed, past the sign on the gate that read, "NO ADMITTANCE BEYOND FENCE," and stood deliberately next to Wheeler. It didn't matter what limits they pushed since they'd become criminals—not ten minutes prior—they might as well break whatever rules they wanted. The experience made them equal parts bold and skittish.

"There aren't any train tracks in Grant," Harrison repeated Wheeler's earlier declaration. He looked to the left and saw a red antique signal house with a dark barred ticket window.

"This is unreal...."

"How could we have not known about this?" Wheeler asked, breathy and excited.

Although their father grew up in the city, he had lived here with their mother since before the boys were born. He knew the landscape in Grant as well as he was known in the area as a respected builder and land developer. The boys felt sure he had never mentioned there being an old train depot and tracks behind the Main Street shops.

Besides that, Harrison's best friend Luke lived in one of the old Victorian homes beyond the commerce section of town. The boys had played in the backyard since before they could toddle. Gazing down the straight track that ran to the north, Harrison knew that they would inevitably have discovered the rails, which would travel through the forest of weedy trees bordering the property. Tracks are permanent. None of this made any sense.

"Look at this," Wheeler called.

He and the Great Dane were making their way down the curved platform to a steel staircase that led to an overhead footbridge. The other two followed, rattling their way up and looking down on the railroad, about thirty feet below. On the opposite side was a rock cliff and a locked gate.

Glancing back from where they had come, Harrison counted the rooftops of his town. It was all there. And somewhere to the southwest was his house, where his parents waited for him and his brother to return. When he looked that way, he saw that the tracks curved sharply to the west, toward the mountains. That wind of adventure gently demanded his attention, but he forced his eyes back to the rear view of Grant.

The windowless backs of the bakery, hardware store, antique market, bookshop, and café were painted blue, red, green, and ivory, respectively, with faded lettering and rusted fire escapes. He could make out the top of his father's office parallel to the first line of shops.

That's when Harrison made a connection. From on high, it looked like he was surveying the small-scale replica of Grant in his cellar. The tracks and the train station materialized in the same layout—parallel Main Street!

Lampposts that bordered the cobblestone road in front of the alley were lit, which would have seemed odd had he considered it. As far as he knew, the back of the commercial downtown didn't see much traffic. He was too baffled by the real-life discovery of his father's train set, however, to question unnecessary lighting.

"I wonder how long it's been abandoned?" Maggie asked, mystified, looking down over the railing and noticing the cobwebs between the bars on the ticket window. As soon as she finished her musing, a two-part whistle was heard coming down the track from the north—like an objection (*har-rumph!*) to her presumptuous accusation that this station might be out of service.

Harrison narrowed his eyes at the blue fog that enveloped the tracks in the direction of the whistle. He saw the steam first—it was blacker than the evening that was settling with the disappearance of the sun. Then from the smoke emerged an old-fashioned steam locomotive, easy to see in the dusk for its brilliant golden color.

"Am I tripping?" Wheeler asked uneasily, and the dog started suddenly across the bridge, back in the direction from which they came.

"We need to roll," Harrison decided, as the train was coming closer to the station and slowing down. He grabbed the other two by the shoulders and pushed them across the bridge, following the dog's lead.
Five pairs of legs thundered down the steps ahead of the train's approach. When it hit the platform, the dog didn't stop but ran back across the road toward the alley. Having been abandoned by their escort, Harrison led his cohorts across the wooden planks toward the old signal house door. It opened willingly without so much as a creak.

Once inside, the brothers peered out the window of the closed door to check out the gold engine, which was pulling a line of red coaches, as it braked to a surprisingly soundless stop.

"This is what hot dog man was talking about," Wheeler whispered.

"We're not getting on any train," Harrison maintained, knowing that was exactly what Wheeler would want to do. "We'll just wait it out here for a while."

"Where is here, Harrison? You know this isn't really Grant. There's no railroad anywhere near our town. Where are we?"

Harrison didn't know. "Of course it's Grant," he said with feigned authority. After all, he saw the town with his own eyes. It was just . . . slightly . . . surreal. "We're just on the other side of Main Street."

"What train would stop in our town?" Wheeler protested.

Harrison didn't answer but continued to stare out the window, a bit worried about a chance encounter with departing passengers. Was this considered trespassing? Would they be turned in to the law? What sort of passengers rode this secret train anyway? Was it a spy train?

Meanwhile Maggie's eyes searched the dark waiting room. She made out rows of old wooden benches that could have doubled as church pews had it not been for the wooden dividers, which marked individual seats and also served as arm rests. There was another barred window on the wall to the left, identical to the one outside, and a door beside it that led into the booth where the ticket agent would sell train passage. She couldn't see another exit besides the door they had come through.

Her hands shielded the front pocket of her hooded sweater. She turned back to the boys, who were still peeking out at the train.

"I don't have a good feeling about this," she spoke to their backs. For all their focused attention, they barely acknowledged her.

"Don't worry. I'll get you out," Harrison said half-heartedly, still fascinated by the plot they had tumbled into.

The light outside disappeared as the dark casually poured over the scene, like coffee from a kettle, matching the interior of the unlit station house. But not even the fade of day could diminish the gleam of that golden engine. Strings of light bulbs hung in arcs from the ceiling over the platform, like widely-spaced jack-o-lantern teeth, being reflected in the locomotive's boiler, which threw the beams back into the boys' eyes, temporarily blinding them.

Inexplicably, the lights in the signal house flickered on.

Maggie screamed.

6. TIME TRAVELERS

She backed into the two Bentley brothers, who, blinking under the abrupt hum of the overhead fluorescents, spun around to face a peculiar man in the waiting room. He was wearing dull striped denim overalls and an engineer's cap. He half-smiled at them, sending a benevolent wave of wrinkles up to his eye on the one side.

Everything about the man echoed the past, including his wide-eyed, flinty stare. He seemed gentle, nonetheless. Harrison tried to study his antique-style clothing and scuffy black boots, but it was almost impossible to look away from the man's full, blue, all-seeing eyes.

"What're you kids doin' here?" the engineer asked. "It's gettin' late now. I expect your momma will be lookin' for you before long." It was not a reprimand; his voice was smooth and friendly.

The reminder of his mother made Harrison momentarily panic. Wheeler, however, seemed untroubled by both the man and that their parents might be worried about them.

Harrison cleared his throat, but he still sounded

hoarse when he finally spoke. "We're not real sure what we're doing here. What is this?"

"It's a train station, son."

At that Wheeler bravely spoke up, remembering Harold's instructions. "We're supposed to get on that train out there—"

Harrison kicked his brother in the ankle and narrowed his eyes to say, *I'm supposed to do the talking, little brother.*

Wheeler flinched, reached one hand down to rub his injury, but otherwise ignored Harrison. "Do you know where it's going?" he asked the man.

"Nowhere you wanna go, I'm sure of that," the engineer chuckled.

Maggie remained flush with Harrison's side. "He was not in here when we came in," she whispered through her teeth.

The man leaned his head back and called at the ticket window. "Dot!"

A moment later the door to the booth opened softly, and a woman in a plaid brown dress and stockings stepped in, like she had been waiting behind the door all that time. She came to stand next to the engineer. Their faces wore the burden of a plain yet demanding life.

The shock of finding people in this desolate place wore off, and when his mind grew keen again, Harrison studied the pair. Except for the man's blue eyes, they looked like they had stepped out of a sepia photograph from the Great Depression era. They were almost colorless. The woman's hair was pulled back and wrung into a knot that was held with pins.

It was her hair that reminded Harrison of a conversation he had overheard when his uncle Jim was sharing a story with his dad. Jim had recently visited the Pentagon and encountered a couple in the corridor, who were dressed in old-fashioned formal wear. He was particularly impressed by the woman's hair, which was elaborately piled and twisted up high, like a popular movie-star hairstyle from the 1940s.

"You know what I think?" Jim had said, emphatically. "I think the government uses time travel."

When Harrison's father had raised his eyebrows, Jim continued. "Well, how do you explain people like that walking around the Pentagon? You should have seen the looks on their faces! You can't recreate that with makeup and wardrobe. They looked lost!"

Maybe the Mighty Midget Kitchen was a portal to the past, Harrison speculated. Perhaps to this couple, it was him that looked lost—like the people at the Pentagon. Just because Grant didn't have any train tracks in Harrison's lifetime, didn't mean that it hadn't once been a stop on the line.

"I'm Curtis. We live in the apartment upstairs," the engineer explained. He took off his hat, revealing short silver hair. Neither of them made any attempt to reach out and shake hands. "Dot's the station agent. She's making supper. Why don't you all stay with us 'til your trouble passes?"

Ah, he had guessed their situation. Harrison

winced again at the unwelcome reminder of their problems.

"The roast ought to be done now," Dot said evenly. As she spoke, the delicious flavor of roast beef floated into the room. Harrison weakened at the smell. His deliberations started to fade, and he forgot about the art festival, Harold and the Mighty Midget, and time travel altogether. All he wanted at that moment was a portion of that meal.

"I am hungry," Wheeler said. "Will that train wait for us?"

"No, Wheeler," Maggie said loudly, startling herself and the others. "Um, we have takeout," she added more cautiously, still clutching at Harrison's arm.

The man spoke up. "Look, you all do not want to get on that train."

All three kids stared at him, waiting for further explanation.

"Follow me then. You can see for yourself."

Curtis left Dot behind and started out the door. Then turning back, he smiled. "C'mon," he beckoned to the kids.

The boys followed him out the door, trailed by Maggie who was right on Harrison's heels.

The four stopped reverentially at the engine. Curtis pulled a wrench out of his cargo pocket. He knelt down and began to tinker with something on one of the wheels. There was a black handkerchief halfway hanging out of his back pocket.

The night air mixed with the strong odor of burning coal revived Harrison's senses. As curious as he was to know what had happened when they crossed into the alley, he knew he was responsible for his brother and this girl, they being younger. He must get them back home.

A wild breeze blew around the body of the train and into their faces. Maggie's teeth chattered.

"This here is the train to The Highlands. The journey there is . . . well, rough. Downright dangerous, to be truthful." Curtis looked up sternly from the wheels as he gave this warning, shaking the wrench at them.

Harrison felt it was time to speak. "Look, I don't know really where we are, or how we got here. I don't like the idea of getting on this train to—The Highlands or wherever. I've never heard of The Highlands. Unless you mean Scotland. And if that's the case, I seriously doubt this train can get us there. All I know is that something strange is going down. When we left the Mighty Midget Kitchen—"

"Har-ri-son," Maggie interrupted, enunciating the syllables of his name and narrowing her eyes. "We have got to get on that train! Harold said so. He packed us food and everything. There are bad people in Grant chasing us, and we have no where else to go. . . ." Her tirade dissolved into a stream of distraught Spanish.

Harrison looked apologetically at Curtis and smiled. "I'm sorry. She really can get too excited sometimes."

"This is nonsense," said Curtis, suddenly sounding angry, "and I'll show you why." He stood and charged down the platform. He stopped at the first passenger car and pointed the wrench at the arched windows. "You see!"

The kids ran after him—stomping clumsily down the wooden planks—and stopped behind his upheld arm.

Maggie gasped.

"What are they?" Wheeler asked.

The light from inside the coaches glowed in the glass, simultaneously casting light to the platform and distinctly illuminating the interior. Inside, standing erectly, were people. Well, perhaps not people. They looked like people . . . except that they were perfect and very still. Like mannequins. And they were taller than most people. Men and women of all races—the car was packed with them. They wore Western-style coats, ties, and hats—even the females.

But their appearance was not what Harrison first noticed; he was dreadfully aware of their massive weapons. Swords and bows and spears and shields. A crease formed in the bridge of his nose.

"Soldiers," Curtis answered, "of a race of giants. On their way to the war in The Highlands."

7. CATCHING THE TRAIN

"I need to get us back to Grant right now," Harrison said adamantly. He wanted answers and, had he been alone, he would have seen this out, but he was thinking about Wheeler and Maggie and their safety.

"This *is* Grant, sonny." It was Dot. She materialized unexpectedly beside them.

"That's right," Curtis took over. "Your parents, Cort and Annie Bentley, live a mile and a half from here." He motioned with his eyes. "The downtown is just across the alley there. Mr. Walker owns the hardware store, the Randolphs run the café. . . ."

Harrison relaxed and turned fuzzy at the mention of his parents' names. He supposed they didn't time travel after all. Curtis seemed trustworthy, and his face was so friendly. Dot was very serious but also non-threatening. Something about them seemed familiar. It wasn't as if they could read his thoughts . . . but maybe they were good at guessing—like they knew what he needed to hear. It was comforting.

Meanwhile, Maggie examined the outside of the signal house, still trying to make sense of Curtis's and

Dot's sudden presence in the vacant waiting room. She noticed the steel staircase that led to a short landing and second-story entrance. That must be the couple's apartment, she thought. There were no lights behind the curtained windows.

The train whistled. Like a horse held back by invisible reins, it wanted to roll but it reluctantly remained, spitting out steam instead.

"If you get on that train, you may not come back," Curtis warned.

Dot softened the approach a bit, without smiling. "It's warm in the signal house. C'mon back inside."

Harrison just wanted it all to go away. He wanted to buy the required dairy product for the quiche and get himself and his brother back home.

Wait. "How did you know my parents' names?" Harrison wondered aloud.

"Well, it's a small town, you know—" Curtis started.

"No, we don't know you," Wheeler accused. "It is a small town, so we would know you. And you are not from Grant."

Then Maggie joined in. "Neither of you were in the signal house when we came in. I was looking. And to get there from your apartment, you would have had to use the outside stairs and the door that the boys were standing against!"

The fog in Harrison's head cleared. Here he was supposed to protect Maggie, and yet he hadn't been listening to her this whole time. Something undeniably strange had happened when they exited the downtown kitchen. Maybe Grant wasn't the safest place for them at the moment . . . but this situation hardly seemed preferable.

"Look out now," Curtis exclaimed sardonically. "We're just tryin' to tell you what's best for you."

The train started to chug forward. Maggie looked at Harrison and mouthed, "Let's go." When she looked desperate like that, he apparently had no choice but to go against his better judgment and give her what she wanted.

"Okay," Harrison said to the man and woman, "thank you for your concern and hospitality. But I don't see that we have any other choice but to go." He was pinching Wheeler's jacket as he slowly backed away. Maggie was still plastered to his left side. "We're going to get on now."

Dot's and Curtis's expressions turned aggressive.

"We are not letting you on that train, son," Curtis growled.

At that moment, he and Dot lunged forward with smooth martial skill. It was so fast, in fact, that in a blink the boy was held firmly by Curtis. Dot possessed Maggie in her bony-fingered grasp. With one arm locked around Harrison, Curtis stretched his other hand for Wheeler, who jumped out of reach.

"Run!" Maggie screamed at him.

"No, don't!" Harrison countered, wriggling against Curtis's iron arm.

In a flash Wheeler was thumping down the platform. He jumped on the back balcony of the first passenger car as it left the depot and leaned over the side, staring back at them, open-mouthed and desperately wild-eyed. Dread was evident in his face, yet excitement and anticipation were also there in the shape of the boy's mouth.

Harrison wanted to sob. He was breathing hard and struggling to escape from Curtis's grip. He didn't know how to fix this anymore.

Really, could it get any worse in one evening? He was a fugitive from the law. He guessed he had entered some alternate reality. He was being held captive by two creepy, outdated people, who had turned hostile. He was separated from Wheeler, who was riding a train with a crowd of freakishly big people with swords.

There was nothing to do; he was helpless and becoming resigned.

Securely restrained in Curtis's menacing embrace, Harrison was facing Maggie and Dot, whose eyes grew large together. Dot's mouth dropped, and Harrison thought at first that she had howled. He realized then, however, that they stared beyond him. He turned his head to look, as did his captor.

Two massive coyotes stood on the platform. Curtis gasped and released Harrison. Dot immediately did the same of Maggie.

The coyotes lowered their heads and the closer rumbled an unfriendly growl. The vocal one was black and difficult to discern if it weren't for the glint of the lights reflected in its eye. When it caught Harrison's attention, he thought its angry grimace changed to amusement—like it would wink at him.

Harrison recognized that their villains had vanished with the threat from the coyotes. Getting rid of that pair had been easy enough, but now what to do about these two new predators?

Maggie crossed herself quickly. Despite the two monsters facing him, it registered in Harrison's mind when he observed her signing that, for Maggie, a higher presence was real, not a possibility. He remembered her family's diligent attendance at St. Mary's mass on Sundays. She requested divine protection then—trying to remember the patron saint for animal attacks (was it Vitus?)—not knowing that she already had it.

"C'mon, Maggie," Harrison called. She cautiously edged close to him.

He wasn't sure what to do, though. He knew for certain they would not be going back in the signal house. That feisty burro from the farm might have come in handy, but Harrison wasn't confident that little Dudley could handle two of these oversized beasts. It would even be some comfort if the Great Dane were to make a timely reappearance.

Oddly, the coyotes also appeared undecided, like they were waiting for Harrison to make up his mind. One glanced at the other and took a couple of tentative steps toward the humans. The other followed, fixing Harrison straight in the eye, as if to say that the choice was an obvious one. It was time to go; Harrison knew

THE HIGHLANDS TUNNEL

that much.

He could see the train still on the tracks ahead. Wheeler was on that train!

Although he was doubtful about whether or not they could outrun coyotes, he decided to try for it. What other option was there? He grabbed Maggie's hand and they sprinted down the platform.

The coyotes started after them. Harrison and Maggie jumped down to the tracks and fled after the train with the animals in pursuit.

Running again, Harrison thought, annoyed. He glanced back, taking in great gulps of air through his mouth. The coyotes were effortlessly keeping pace. Looking ahead he saw that they were going to make it . . . that was as long as the creatures didn't pick up speed and overtake them. And he knew they could if they wanted to.

But they didn't. Instead, that unconventional little coyote pack in pursuit made them run fast—even Maggie in her ballet shoes—and the kids were gaining on the train. What waited for them there or at its destination, Harrison did not know, but at least he would be where Wheeler was.

8. CROSSING THE BORDER

Harrison caught the ladder on the back of the last car and pulled himself on. Maggie had almost made it, but she stumbled. A coyote bared its teeth and came near to nipping her leg, motivating her to leap back up and close the rest of the distance.

Harrison helped her from the small deck on the back of the caboose, grabbing her by the arms until she got her footing. They stood together watching the coyotes slow to a jog, until they finally halted. The coyotes did not look tired at all, but rather pleased about the run.

Maybe, Harrison thought, their intention was not to catch up to them after all, but rather to give chase. Like a lazy dog in a field full of rabbits. The boy and girl tried but couldn't think badly of the beasts . . . even the one that had attempted to bite Maggie.

Watching the animals disappear around a bend in the tracks, Harrison and Maggie—who wrapped her long arms around her chest—concentrated on catching their breath. Then in unison they turned heedfully to the back of the caboose.

THE HIGHLANDS TUNNEL

The inside was illuminated, and it appeared to be a sort of observation car with lots of windows . . . and it was empty. No Wheeler, though that didn't surprise Harrison since his brother had jumped on the first in the line of coaches. And no giants, much to their relief.

They entered timidly and inspected their surroundings. It was quite luxurious, with teal velvet seats, fancy ironwork, heavy red curtains, and a roaring fire in a glossy woodstove at the front.

After a pause, they were seated on a bench together letting their hearts slow. Maggie pulled out the food bag Harold had packed them. They devoured two roast beef sandwiches and fried cheese sticks, all the while remembering Dot's mysterious roast cooking in the unseen upstairs oven of the signal house. They wondered if the menu selection was a coincidence.

Maggie was eyeing Wheeler's portion, so Harrison split it between them.

Poor Wheeler. He was always hungry. Hopefully the giant people could feed him—if they ate food, which seemed unlikely. In the old stories, giants ate . . . people. That was an unwelcome thought. These giants, however, looked as stiff as statues . . . and statues didn't eat at all.

So Curtis and Dot turned out to be bad guys. . . . That seemed to Harrison reason enough not to trust the people on the train either. If they were indeed soldiers (which seemed likely, judging by the weapons they carried), whose side were they on? And what war were they fighting?

Harrison was agitated by the turn of events. He didn't know where Wheeler was, who these tall people were, why they transported weapons, or where this train was going. He didn't appreciate unanswered questions, particularly when he was so out of the realm of his ordinary lifestyle. This was danger and mystery unfiltered. All the things he used to pursue. But being here, and being responsible for not only himself but also Wheeler and Maggie, felt frustrating instead of entertaining.

Maggie studied his wary expression and thoughtfully commented. "I guess I'm more used to this sort of thing. Running . . . hiding . . . sneaking around, you know."

Harrison wasn't looking at her.

"I'm not supposed to tell anyone this, but," she paused for effect, "I didn't come here on an airplane. I mean, to the States."

"No kidding, Maggie," he said sarcastically. Although he had never heard anyone say it so directly, he knew she was telling the truth about this. Hers was certainly not the only family who had immigrated this way.

"My father carried me across the river and over the wall on his back. I was sick—"

"Then why did he do that?" Harrison snapped, cutting her off.

She pouted briefly. "Remember I told you he was a boxer. He had won a lot of money. There were these bad men in a gang—"

Harrison interrupted again. "I don't understand then why he risked your safety to take you with him. It would have been safer for you if he had walked away." Her stories used to amuse him, but now he was tired and irritated by her lies.

"Because he wouldn't leave me."

"Is it better then that you almost died in the desert?"

She didn't answer that. Instead she shoved her hands into her front pocket.

A moment later, Maggie retorted. "I don't understand why you don't believe me. Back at the art festival, you didn't believe me either. You wouldn't stand up for me. Bad things happen to people, Harrison. There are bad people in the world, and not just outside of Grant either." She was riled then. "What if he had left me in Mexico? Those men would have come for me. He would have given them anything for me, but they would have killed me anyway!"

And just like that, Harrison felt like scum. How did she make him so angry one minute, tender the next, and then guilty after that? She could be very convincing when she was worked up.

Her fingers looked to be fidgeting in her front pocket. He wanted to hold her hand, to let her know he was sorry that he was a jerk. He wanted her to know that it would be okay and that he would protect her.

He reached into the front pocket.

His fingers brushed hers and she looked at him. Her intensely dark eyes softened with his touch. He knew she would forgive him for being bad tempered. But then he felt something other than her hand knocking against his knuckles. He grasped it and realized what it was even before he'd pulled it out to look.

There in its leather cover was the stolen knife with the painted handle.

"I don't believe this!" Harrison nearly shouted.

"Harrison, please! Let me explain. . . ."

He stood up and practically threw the knife back at her. He headed for the front of the car. She held the knife over her chest, as though he had stabbed her with it.

"Where are you going? Please don't leave me!" Maggie begged.

"I'm going to find my brother," he barked, feeling completely stupid and used.

THE HIGHLANDS TUNNEL

9. BIRDS

After he released this last communication, Harrison would not look at her wounded face anymore. He was determined to reach the front exit with his emotions intact. But a loud thud caused him to turn his head back reluctantly.

Maggie shrieked at the blackened window. Clawing at the glass by Maggie's head was a colossal hawk-like bird. Its wingspan covered the length of the window—easily six feet of feathered force. The scraping created shudders that ran from their toes up to their necks, and Maggie covered her ears as she backed into Harrison.

Then a second bird hit the back door. Instead of falling, however, it swooped up, retreated, and tried the door again. Harrison couldn't say how he had figured, but he just knew they were Dot and Curtis. *I should have known we hadn't seen the last of them*, Harrison chided himself. It was in that moment of dread that he fully accepted the possibility of this being a supernatural realm. It was the birds that convinced him—he had taken a train into his own personal nightmare.

Ugh, how he hated birds! When he was a child, a

rooster had pecked a hole through his shoe and into his foot. It kept getting infected and left a scar when the wound finally healed. And then, there was the biology teacher who brought her pet parakeets to class. They fluttered around the room during her lectures, randomly perching on students' heads. Harrison spent the class hour projecting silent but violent threats to the birds to stay out of his hair!

The present feathered fiend thrashed at the back door again, but this time the traitor unlatched. The bird soared into the car, followed by its partner. Harrison stared directly into the one hawk's large blue eyes. Their talons spread, their beaks opened, to capture Harrison and Maggie, who luckily ducked under and fled out the open door. The birds screamed, gracelessly made to turn around, and pursued the boy and girl, who were once again at a loss about how to escape this latest quandary. The wings beat at their heads and a gnarled claw scratched Harrison's face. The fowl wanted the kids off that train, and they were going to harass them until they either jumped or fell.

"Up here," Harrison ordered, gesturing to Maggie to climb the ladder to the rooftop. He assumed they would find a way down on the other side of the car.

Once on top, they carefully tread the length of the coach. Unlike the movies, there would be no running on the rooftop of this traveling train. Especially in the dark while giant hawks swooped down at their heads in a terrific campaign of abuse. Maggie held her arms protectively over her hair, but Harrison held his out for balance.

There was also the shifting jolt of the cars and a forceful wind that made their shoes slide. The cold moist air and rushing sound on either side of the train indicated water. As it happened, a wide misty river cascaded below in the cloudy moonlight, but neither traveler could stomach a peek. The notion of what was under the tracks and how far down made Harrison feel like he was going to throw up. Was it the Potomac River? Harrison thought the train had chugged toward the west, but perhaps it had traveled north first. He was a bit disoriented at the moment.

Meanwhile, the train clattered over the bridge at a steady pace, the trusses rhythmically rushing by.

Of course we are walking on top of the train, he was thinking. *What else could happen tonight?*

One hawk landed behind them on the roof of the car, and it followed in their wake, hopping and flapping, shooing them toward the edge.

When he came to the end, Harrison could not find the ladder he had assumed—and hoped—was there. He fumbled with his hand under the eaves to be sure his eyes weren't missing it in the night. Ahead, in the vague moonlight, he spied the ladder on the next coach.

He would unfortunately have to ask Maggie to jump. She looked afraid. Although two minutes ago he was furious with her, now he wanted to hold her hand again. But making the jump together would dash the odds of clearing the space.

THE HIGHLANDS TUNNEL

"Like this, Maggie," Harrison said, checking first to see if he were the upcoming target of the aerial attack. He took several steps backward, then picked up the pace for the jump forward. The car rattled and clunked when he landed on his palms and knees. He turned around and nodded at Maggie, and she nodded back but hesitated.

He searched the sky again for the dive-bombing hawk. The moon was like a steady flashlight, muted and blurred in the fog. Dot or Curtis was circling overhead, coming closer with each spiral and uttering an odd stuttered quack. Their shrill squawking suggested a threat, but Harrison couldn't yet see what it was.

He turned around and glimpsed a tall dark shape on top of the coach ahead. The moon outlined the figure's silhouette in silvery fuzz.

It appeared to be a giant man. He was holding a bow that was as tall as Harrison and aiming an arrow at the sky.

Beyond him, Harrison saw that the train had made it to the Western mountain range, which looked like an endless dark-blue shadow. The steam from the locomotive floated across its base. A hulk of mountain faced the train, but the rails met it straight on. A tunnel, Harrison realized.

Now, he had seen enough movies to know that the tops of trains generally ran an inch or so below the tops of tunnels. Whether that was reality or not didn't matter. That and the ghostly archer settled it: they must get off the roof of the train.

"Maggie! Come on! Jump!"

She was turned away from him and kicking at the hawk, which was trying to peck at her feet.

There was a reverberated twang and swoosh behind him as the bowman let the arrow fly. Harrison was unable follow the arrow by sight but heard the force of it when it hit the bird in flight. The wounded hawk fell without a beat of its wings. The second bird ended the pursuit on its feet and lifted from the rooftop into the air. The pluck of the bowstring signaled the release of a second arrow, which succinctly struck the other hawk, either Curtis or Dot.

Like a pitiful last-ditch effort to hurt him, a feather from the felled fowl hit Harrison's face, brushing the raw wound. He touched his hand to where the bird's claw had cut him and it burned in response.

This made it twice in one day that he had been a predator's prey. There may be a first time for everything, but did it ever happen in succession like this?

Surprising himself, he almost laughed with relief. Harrison had never had the inclination to hunt, and he hated the thought of an animal suffering . . . but he knew these were not natural birds, and he was happy to be rid of them.

The comfort was short-lived, however. There was the approaching tunnel and the more immediate danger . . . the giant was quickly striding toward him with bow in hand.

THE HIGHLANDS TUNNEL

10. THE CONDUCTER

"Maggie, come on!" he shouted. But then Harrison stilled, as he felt a large presence hovering at his back.

"Ah, here are my stowaways," came a deep and lyrical voice. Harrison looked up—a long way from on his knees—into a handsome chocolate-colored face. He could see his own shocked expression reflected in the Goliath man's dark eyes.

His long legs comfortably cleared the space between the two rooftops. Maggie gasped, but allowed him to pick her up like a marionette (although he didn't ask permission) and cross back to Harrison's car.

The giant terrified Harrison, but Maggie seemed calmer in his arms. He knew Maggie well enough to know that she would fight back—even a giant—if she sensed real danger.

Harrison stood at the man's approach. He was grateful that the giant didn't pick him up as well, although he easily could have.

"Let us take our seats, shall we? We are approaching the tunnel and I am not sure we have not seen the last of those two scavengers."

With a solemn mien but a good-humored voice, he didn't sound *too* concerned about the hawks. The statement confused Harrison because he was convinced the arrows had killed the birds, if not rendered them flightless. Of course, if they were Dot and Curtis, he supposed they could change forms again, and maybe they couldn't be killed or injured.

"Go ahead, quickly." The man urged Harrison to climb down the ladder.

He did so and watched as the tall archer descended, holding Maggie at his side, his bow strung over his shoulder. It reminded Harrison of King Kong climbing the Empire State Building with his tiny woman in hand.

Setting Maggie down on the platform, their escort opened the door for them. He didn't ask or force them to follow, but bemused and battered, they jogged to keep up with his long rapid strides down the aisle of the passenger coach. His head and shoulders hunched so as not to hit the dangling light fixtures.

Unlike his first impression of Curtis and Dot, Harrison's instincts told him to be afraid. The man was probably seven feet tall—too big to be a ghost. Characters this tall fell more in the monster category of mythical creatures. He wore dark trousers with a thick belt, black boots, collared shirt with the sleeves rolled up, and a black Fedora.

Harrison did not know what else to do but go after him. He hadn't done anything Harrison could object to, and he must know where to find Wheeler.

The giant man opened another door at the front of the car, and they set foot in a little entryway with an open window on one side and an outside exit with steps on the other.

As the man was ducking through yet another door to another coach, the hawk with the blue eyes flew through the open window and plowed into Maggie.

It felt like slow motion to Harrison. All in the same instant she fell backward out the door with the hawk angling upward and out into the blackness. In a reflexive action, Harrison's hand shot out and grasped Maggie's sweater. They both tumbled onto the short stairs. Harrison shut his eyes and braced himself to hit the speeding ground. When he peeked, he could make out the timbers of the railroad charging by underneath.

Whereas he was facing the tracks, Maggie was gawking at Harrison's face. Her eyes held a sense of bewilderment—like she was surprised he had reached for her. Thief or not, she must know he didn't intend to let her fall.

Am I such a monster? he thought, looking her straight in the eyes. *I just don't like to be lied to, that's all.* He hoped she could interpret his thoughts, as he assumed they would be his last.

But before they could topple out, a powerful mainstay had reached out and caught him—it held onto Maggie, too. Harrison didn't let go of her but recognized the sculpted arms and fingers like onyx gripping him and the girl. One of the hawks attacked, trying but failing to clutch the bowman's stone-like arms.

Harrison quaked at the giant's growl.

"This is my train, and they are under my protection now. Now away with you before I shoot you again!" he thundered in his regal African accent.

The birds cawed and flapped, seemingly frozen in air but keeping with the speed of the train. They did not seem daunted by the threat of arrows. They must have supposed the man had his hands full keeping Harrison and Maggie safely on the train to try with his archery aim again.

"Why don't you just shoot them?" Maggie blared over the sound of the wind and the clacking wheels.

"The tunnel is approaching," the man repeated.

"Well, can't you stop the train?" He had said it was his train, Harrison remembered.

"Oh, no. You cannot make any unscheduled stops on this train. Besides, it is important that we make it through that tunnel. We must get you out of the Crossing as soon as possible. It is very difficult to keep you safe here."

Harrison didn't know what the Crossing was, but he liked the way the "r" rolled in the giant's mouth.

"Let us go. The tunnel," he reminded. Maggie obediently uncurled herself out from under Harrison and stood to go.

Remaining on the floor of the deck, his head hanging out the side of the train, Harrison allowed the frigid wind to pummel his face. He craned his neck to look ahead, straight into the black emptiness of the tunnel, which was about two hundred feet away and closing.

The stone blocks that framed the chasm were gray, cracked, and cold. Fallen tree branches and disorderly weeds all but blocked the entrance, and the mountainous boulders beside it were covered with moss. Oddly, a large "NO TRESPASSING" sign crowned the arch. "TRESPASSING IS STRICTLY PROHIBITED. VIOLATORS WILL BE PROSECUTED," it warned.

"Or pecked to death," Harrison muttered under his breath, resentfully revising its message.

As in respect for the law of the sign, the hawks cried one last objection and flapped away . . . or so it seemed.

And then Harrison, still half-hanging from the train, saw Curtis materialize in the mist, standing with arms folded across his chest beside the entrance to the tunnel. He glared wickedly at the boy with his electric blue, laser-beam eyes.

In shock, Harrison shouted something that sounded like *"Cha!"*

He kicked his legs in a hasty attempt to get up and put distance between him and the shape-shifting train engineer. The archer helped by pulling him up from the steps. He picked Maggie up again and crossed the couplings to the next coach.

Harrison followed close to the great man, gripping the banister as he crossed the space. He didn't care what came next, he just wanted to be inside that car and safe from hawks . . . or humans pretending to be hawks—or was it hawks pretending to be human? As if they were actually hawks or human! Whichever it was or wasn't, he was grateful that Maggie didn't seem to have glimpsed the final display of their menace.

The giant opened the next door and, for the first time, he smiled, his teeth like starlight in his dark face.

"Do not be afraid," he said softly as the train began its haunting whistle-song.

And then . . . .

11. Darkness

. . . the tunnel.

Streaks of light flashed—inside the tunnel, outside the train—but they could see nothing. And although it was dark, Harrison felt illuminated.

It was obvious that something was happening. If they had time traveled before and not known it, they understood now that they were getting even farther away—not only from Grant but from their world altogether.

The time in the tunnel was only seconds, but during that lapse of darkness, Harrison readied himself for what lay ahead on the other side of the tunnel. He would have to be brave, and he would have to think of Wheeler and Maggie first. They must return safely even if Harrison didn't. He would do whatever it took for that to happen.

His anger at Maggie was background noise that decreased in volume, becoming more muted the further his resolve strengthened. Perhaps it was seeing her handled like a child by the giant that had softened him. Or her expression when he had caught her, confused about his intention, her head inches away from the ground.

He was proud of that act. Even though had it not been for the tall man's quick reflexes, they both would have fallen overboard, at least he had reached out and caught her. He was not so certain about the quality of his behavior downtown, however—helping her escape when he should have minded his own business. Noble intent, yes. Intelligent decision . . . perhaps not.

It may have been her fault that they were in this predicament, but Harrison chose there in the darkness to accept the circumstances and follow through.

No, he would not bail out on this mission.

12. COWBOY GIANTS

A loud hurrah erupted in the compartment when the car broke into the light. It wasn't bright daylight, but it wasn't dark night yet. It was evening—sunset—the same time of day as when they had walked away from the Mighty Midget Kitchen.

The floor of the car shook when the passengers—these towers of living sculpture—stomped their weapons, laughing and cheering for triumph.

When the brief riot ended, Harrison inspected the inhabitants of the coach. Their celebration contrasted with their sober century-old clothing. Some looked like cowboys and others like lawmen. The women, as well, although there were no pioneer dresses here. No skirts or petticoats or aprons. The females dressed for a gun fight, too.

As fierce as their appearance would imply, there was nothing rough about them. No scars or stubble or dimples or wrinkles. Smooth, fluid, still.

Where was Wheeler? Harrison started to panic when he realized his brother wasn't in the car. He *had* caught the train. What if the terrorist hawks had knocked him off somewhere in the Crossing?

"My brother?" he questioned frantically. Turning his head back and forth, Harrison shouted at no one in particular.

"Wheeler is in the dining car," answered the dark man. "He was quite hungry. Do not worry, I will bring him to you . . . if I can pull him away."

Harrison almost relaxed at that news, except that then all eyes were aimed on him.

Apparently his plea had attracted the attention of the fellow travelers. Their chiseled faces—every color from ivory and sunlight to wheat and earth, but no two alike—stared at him. He looked nervously at their oversized weapons and gulped. These wouldn't be mere props or accessories if they didn't match the era of their costumes. Nobody had ever pictured a cowboy with a sword.

Harrison kept blinking at them, not sure if he should salute or put up his hands or what.

Their gaze felt anxious initially. They were hesitant, almost as if they were suspicious of these human teenagers.

Harrison noticed Maggie gripping the stolen knife in her sweater pocket. What was she thinking? Did she intend to wound these steel giants with her small weapon? Despite the seriousness of the situation, Harrison coughed out a laugh.

And with that, they smiled back.

Only a couple at first, and then it kindled—about twenty-five perfect smiles beaming their way. It seemed the light in the car grew brighter. And when Maggie ushered a quiet hello, they laughed and approached, not bothering to take turns. Living art forms, as they seemed, were quite jolly. They clapped Harrison on the shoulder and kissed Maggie's cheeks. Welcomes resounded in many languages.

Harrison and Maggie couldn't help but smile likewise and return their touches.

"*Gracias,*" Maggie giggled when she found a couple of Spanish-speaking giants. "*Estoy feliz de estar aqui.*"

"*Je suis enchante,*" Harrison contributed, using the little bit of appropriate *Français* acquired from his Parisian grandmother. Mostly at home he spoke gutter French, which he didn't always understand and which he picked up from his father, who frequently swore under his breath. Calling a giant a bad name in French was probably a poor way to begin the human-supernatural relationship, so he left off at the greeting.

The crowd gracefully parted then, still exclaiming, as the dark one escorted Wheeler to Harrison and Maggie.

Ah, the relief! Harrison wanted to hug him, but they didn't normally show affection. Instead, he exhaled and punched Wheeler's shoulder.

"Where've you been, little brother? I was so worried."

"Where have *you* been?" Wheeler retorted, rolling his eyes.

"I'll bet you didn't think about me at all," Harrison accused.

THE HIGHLANDS TUNNEL

"I did . . . a little." Wheeler grinned. He patted his stomach with both hands and stretched his arms up toward the ceiling, like he'd finished an excessive holiday meal. "I scored some decent grub."

"This is unbelievable," Harrison whispered as he shook his head and glanced around.

"I know! These guys love the mortals," Wheeler replied enthusiastically.

Whereas normally the sight of his brother would have made Harrison think of his parents . . . surprisingly he didn't. While in the tunnel, he'd resolved to rescue his companions. That was his focus and no other worry or scheme dared to encroach on that.

The cheeriness affected Harrison, too. Perhaps it was the lighting, but he hadn't felt so happy since he could remember. It was like a chemical spreading through his body, erasing the panic and flight-or-fight reflex. The curiosity remained, but it was pleasant, not anxious.

He noticed Wheeler's untied Converse sneakers, and he teasingly cuffed the side of his head.

"You'd better keep your shoes tied and ready to run," he warned.

Wheeler just laughed, and Harrison joined him, even after Wheeler returned the smack with a jab to Harrison's side.

The archer in black approached and introduced himself formally.

"My name is Aubrey," he said with a slight bow. "I am your guide, your guard, your kinsman, et cetera."

He never hesitated or stuttered. The words were born from his mouth as glossy as piano music.

"He's sort of like the conductor," Wheeler interrupted. "Except he isn't taking tickets."

"He is right in that I am to conduct you from the Practice World to The Highlands."

"So it's okay that we jumped on your train?" Maggie ventured shyly.

"Yes, as you can see, you are quite welcome here."

"I have a question," Harrison posed, waiting for Aubrey's permission to continue. "Are we in the past? I mean, what decade is this? Or what century?"

"Oh, do you mean this?" He gestured to his clothes. "No, we are not in the past. This is very much the present. Only time is not marked as such here. This," again he pointed to his wardrobe, "is all for you. Do you like it? The Giver wanted to give you an adventure. The Giver knows precisely what you like."

Harrison stopped a moment to take that in. He squinted his eyes in puzzlement, as he knew no Giver.

"And we're going to a war?"

"Pardon?" It was Aubrey's turn to look confused. "No. We only just returned from the battle. We will not go back again until daybreak."

"Those people at the train station—uh, the hawks. . . ." Harrison said tentatively, stammering at the contradiction and absurdity of it.

"Yes," Aubrey confirmed, nonchalant, with a nod.

"When they were human—or appeared as humans—they said you all were going to the war in The

Highlands."

"Well, they lied." Aubrey shook his head, seeming slightly irritated. "There is no war in The Highlands. It is our camp. And you are correct. They are not human, but they are very good at acting like it. Much better than we are," he laughed. "That is what they do: they lie. Copies—that is what we call them. They cannot come up with anything original." He scowled, looking handsome despite the frown.

How do I know that you are not lying? Harrison wondered skeptically. Still, he was grateful for the explanation. These were important clues to figuring it all out, and Harrison took note, despite his confusion and doubt.

"Copies," Wheeler repeated, sounding disappointed. "Couldn't you come up with something more bad? Those people were wicked."

"You should have seen them in their bird form," Harrison said, gritting his teeth at the recent memory.

Aubrey answered, "Oh, we are not afraid of the Copies." Then, considering for a moment, he revised. "But perhaps you should be."

He paused and looked like he was about to chuckle. "I wasn't afraid of them," Harrison said confidently. "I was more concerned about the coyotes."

"Rightly so," Aubrey agreed with a grin. "What other questions have you thought up? Actually, perhaps I had better start filling you in."

13. QUERIES

Through the windows, like flashes of movie film, they could see that the train was winding up into the mountains. Eventually sporadic vistas opened up, revealing hazy valleys being invaded by the dusk. Countless ridges stacked up in the distance.

The party of four took a seat on two facing benches, conversing and occasionally glimpsing at the scenery. Aubrey sat by himself—the other three squeezed in across from him. His face, although sleek and stony, was warm and elegant. His expression peaceful, authoritative, and regal.

Harrison noticed that Maggie finally seemed still, whereas before she had been trembling for he didn't know how long.

"You said this was your train. How come you can't stop it?" Harrison questioned in a polite tone. He was not afraid of Aubrey anymore but definitely still intimidated.

"This is our train," he explained, including all the cowboy warriors with a wave of his big hand. "It is on a course, a schedule, and that I cannot change."

"Okay . . . but you can take new passengers?"

"As long as they get on in time."

Maggie and Wheeler sat quietly, listening. They seemed content to let Harrison conduct the interview.

"Sorry, you were ready to explain. Why are we on this train?"

Aubrey launched into a summary of recent events. "Well, you entered Harold's diner and exited into the Crossing." Harrison noted that Aubrey knew Harold of the Mighty Midget Kitchen. "You encountered a pair of Copies, who attempted to make you complacent enough to miss the train. When that was not successful, they tried to frighten you. Finally, they attempted to physically restrain you. And then, as you pointed out"—he looked as if he were about to wink—"a couple of wild coyotes scared the Copies away and chased you onto the train."

Oh, we remember all that! Harrison countered mentally. *Okay, fine. Let's work backwards here. . . .* He was plotting. How he wished he had his tape recorder! Maybe he could ask if Maggie had swiped one from the market and hidden it in her front pocket with the knife.

"You know the coyotes," Maggie insisted.

"Yes." Aubrey stopped at that, his face stoic.

Maggie was perceptive—Harrison would give her that.

"But you're not going to tell us where they came from?" Harrison asked.

"No," he shook his head, displaying a brilliant

smile. "You will soon discover."

"The Copies—who—why. . .?" Harrison wasn't sure where to start. "Who are they?"

"Creations of the Unseen Enemy."

"The Unseen. . . ." he couldn't finish.

"Enemy?" Wheeler helped out, enthusiasm apparent in his query.

"Yes, the Unseen cannot be everywhere. The Unseen sends its creatures out to do the bulk of the policing."

The idea of an enemy having its hand in his current situation was not so frightening to Harrison. On the contrary, he was amazed. *How could something so awesome and terrifying be happening to me? When did my life become so cool?*

All at once, the craving for a chase was reborn, like in his dream. Harrison's instincts jumped to pursue the mystery.

The emotion was slightly different from Wheeler's intrigue. His brother was reckless—he had no fear; Harrison recognized the danger—he would need to be extra vigilant to keep him out of trouble.

"Why did the Unseen, or the Unseen's bouncers, not want us to get on the train?" he asked.

"Mmm," Aubrey shook his head and tightened his eyes. "That is another one that you will have to uncover for yourself."

"I've never seen them before, but they seemed familiar. . . ."

"Oh, you know them."

Harrison's eyes widened with surprise and confusion.

"The Copies spend most of their time in the Practice World. That is where you live," he threw in as an aside. "The female, for example. You know her as Mrs. Byrne."

"My physics teacher?" Harrison gasped.

Mrs. Byrne was always on his case about being more responsible, working harder, and owning up to his potential. Harrison's parents loved her. Sure, she was hard to please, but he never suspected that she wasn't human.

"No way! Mrs. Byrne works for the Enemy," Wheeler exclaimed. He was well aware of Harrison's struggle in physics. "Wait 'til I tell Mom and Dad."

"What about Coach Marshall?" Maggie asked.

Aubrey frowned over a ready smile and shook his head.

Harrison had not once really looked at Mrs. Byrne, he realized when he tried to recall her. Her appearance was inconsequential, very much like Dot's. He couldn't even describe her features.

"Her talent is distraction," Aubrey clarified without being asked to.

"Well, that explains all the homework," Harrison said quietly, still baffled. There were bad guys in Grant after all.

"What about the man?" Maggie asked.

"He goes out in various forms, but he mostly loiters in the Crossing until he is needed. He and the female sort of work as a team. He runs back and forth with orders and assists her when necessary. She outranks him."

"But they wouldn't hurt us. . .?" Harrison started to ask.

"Oh, they will kill you if they have to. But not unless they get the orders from the Unseen."

Okay, that was something to pause about. Harrison didn't feel his mouth hanging open.

Aubrey tried to console them, wrinkling his eyebrows. "Only your form, of course. They can only kill your form."

The Unseen Enemy could order his death. Harrison felt cold as he reflected on that information. Were there orders for his life? More importantly, did the Enemy want Wheeler or Maggie killed? This was big. Too big to fully consider at the moment.

When he eventually snapped to, Harrison continued the interrogation. "You shot them, and they fell."

Aubrey scoffed. "They cannot die." He sighed heavily.

His suspicions confirmed, Harrison continued firing off the questions. "The Crossing—what is that?"

"It is in between the Practice World and The Highlands. Just one of the levels of reality."

"Is it dangerous?"

"It can be. But the Practice World is just as perilous. Only things are not quite so disguised in the Crossing. It is peaceful for some, fearful for others."

Back to the original question, Harrison thought. "I

THE HIGHLANDS TUNNEL

know how we got here. *Why* are we here?"

"The Giver wants to show you something."

"Oh," Harrison responded with surprise.

14. THE STORY

"Who is the Giver?"

Harrison remarked that Aubrey had mentioned the Giver before—that the Giver wanted to "give" Harrison an adventure.

"Just as there is an Unseen Enemy, there is an Unseen Giver. The Giver is the essence of all of this." Aubrey waved his hand toward the window. "The artist, you may say, as well as the creation. And although remaining unseen, not undetectable. The Giver loves to manifest, but you must be aware to sense the presence." Astonishingly, Aubrey sighed like a boy in love.

"Great," Harrison said, letting his self-doubt show. "I'm really not that observant."

"The Giver also wants more than to be seen. The Giver wants to be believed."

Maggie and Wheeler had left Harrison and Aubrey alone when two of the other giants, a male and a female, asked if they could give them a tour of the train. Maggie started chattering happily as she walked away arm-in-arm with the woman. She had been rather subdued until the friendly invitation snapped her back

THE HIGHLANDS TUNNEL

to her usual talkative self.

"Well, I think I can about believe anything after today." Then Harrison remembered what Curtis had said. "Why are you at war? And where? In the Crossing?"

"No, in your level."

It took Harrison a moment to realize Aubrey was talking about his world, his home in Grant . . . the Practice World.

"But there hasn't been a war for a couple decades," he objected. "All the soldiers are, like, older than my dad now."

"There is a lot more going on there than you might assume. Your human wars do not even begin to touch the surface of it."

"But we don't see you. I'm sure we would notice you walking down Main Street . . . or in Times Square even."

The mental image made Harrison chuckle.

"We seem to be invisible in the Practice World. No one bothers to look, I suppose, although one would imagine we are hard to miss. It is the Copies and their art of distraction. Animals, children sometimes, the dying. . . . If we need to be seen by others, we must take on other forms.

"If you could really see people for who they are, Harrison, you would be astounded. Your physics teacher, for instance. If you had looked beyond her form, you would have been horrified. Of course, she makes it that way, so that you do not notice her enough to look."

"Why are you fighting in my," he spoke the word

slowly, "level?"

Aubrey's face was grieved. "There was an assassination. . ." he narrowed his eyes before finishing, "plot."

The last word was misleading—like a contradictory afterthought. An assassination plot could be quite different from an assassination.

"Who? Was it successful?" Harrison prompted.

"Yes. And no. Only because it was part of the plan. Someone had to be the sacrifice. Now it looks like we are at the point in which all hope is lost. We have the upper hand, though. I assure you of that. They will not have the victory. I think they know it, too, and that is why their attacks grow so vicious. The Giver loves the mortals, and that is why the Copies persist. They killed him, and it did not work the way they thought, so they try to hurt you. When they hurt you, they hurt him."

When Aubrey used the masculine pronoun, Harrison was even more baffled. He noticed that Aubrey had deliberately not labeled the Giver a he or a she. This was a new character to add to the plot.

"Who did they kill? The Giver? Who is *he*?"

"The Ransom. He is the Sacrifice. He is everything to us. We love him, therefore, we love what he loves."

"And what is that?"

Aubrey grabbed Harrison's arms with two colossal hands and stunned him with an intense stare. His warm grasp created serious pressure, but the hands were not rock-hard as Harrison had assumed. His touch felt soft and tingly, like his fingers sent out a feathery electric current that penetrated the boy's body.

THE HIGHLANDS TUNNEL

Aubrey answered his question emphatically. "You!"

Presumably, Aubrey was referring to the whole of humanity, but the way he looked at him, it seemed to Harrison like he was declaring a commitment to him alone.

"You are on this train for a very special reason. You are important to our fight. You are the reason we get on this train everyday to go to the Practice World. Otherwise, we would stay in The Highlands. It really is lovely here. Excuse me for a moment."

Aubrey let go and was gone in a flash. But Harrison could still feel where his hands had held him.

Their conversation confused Harrison, but the missing pieces only added to the charm of the mystery. Someone had been killed. It obviously wasn't the Giver, because whoever that was still existed to design this journey for Harrison. Whoever the Ransom was, he had been much loved by the warriors. The assassination had started a war in the Practice World, in which Harrison lived. He was important, and it was no accident that he was on the train. He wondered with some readiness if he would be allowed to join the fight against the Unseen and its army of Copies.

The sound of the train was different now—not as urgent but still fast and steady. Rather than chugging ahead, it was being pulled. Like gravity almost . . . but it was more like the machine had feelings for whatever attracted it. Perhaps not *feelings* but something stronger—more like an instinct. The train needed to be home. It was allowing itself to be drawn toward the center, the heart of The Highlands.

Harrison was aware of this phenomenon because his body simulated the train's energy. He was electrically charged, a piece of steel being dragged to a magnet. Like the train, he was content enough to be pulled forward, without guessing what—or who—could be drawing him in.

He thoughtfully stroked his face. His fingertips detected a vertical line of skin that was rough and patchy under his eye—the scratch from the hawk's talon. It should have stung and oozed, being so recently acquired, but it didn't hurt anymore. He looked into the immediate reflection in the window and made out the ghostly image of his face. The wound was sealed, although a scar remained.

THE HIGHLANDS TUNNEL

15. JOURNEY

Aubrey returned and announced with panache, "We are almost at our destination."

Harrison's heart rate accelerated . . . but not for fear.

"Aubrey?" he asked.

"Yes, Harrison?"

"Who are you? I mean—you're not really from Kenya or anything." The last sentence was not a question. The African accent sounded authentic, but Aubrey was so obviously supernatural, not simply foreign.

"No." He smiled.

"And, you're not one of the Copies," Harrison added.

"How do you guess that?" Aubrey asked, amused.

Harrison picked out the most obvious of all the reasons. "Because you're much taller."

Aubrey beamed in response, took a short bow, and declared with sincerity, "I serve the Giver, and I fight for the Ransom. I am a friend. You are safe with me, Harrison Bentley. . . ." His eyes rolled halfway up before he modified the statement. "For now," he added dryly.

This menacing endnote didn't phase Harrison. He was distracted with pleasure by the rolling "r's" in his name as they issued from Aubrey's tongue. He may have just met Aubrey, and one hour ago he had been terrified of him, but since coming out of the tunnel, Harrison wanted never to leave his presence. This being, whatever he was, had expressed emotion—such that Harrison had not received—even from his own father! And it was for him!

"Are you a ghost?" he asked boldly.

Aubrey clicked his tongue. "No, I think ghosts are white." Then he issued a booming laugh that echoed through the car.

The train was slowing, its eager noises shifting to frequent hissing and occasional groans. After a final drawn-out screech, it finally was stopped.

The cowboy warriors left their weapons and exited the coach.

"You may call us Laochs, the Ancient Ones. Known in various cultures as elves, fairy folk, et cetera. Let us go now."

Harrison hesitated. He had so struggled with the decision to get on this train. Might he ought to think before getting out? No. He had already chosen to follow through with the adventure, therefore he would proceed. And he needed to find his charges, of course. Finally he obeyed, exiting the passage and stepping out ahead of Aubrey. He took mental note of this new word: *Laoch*. It mixed in his mind with other words like Ransom, Giver, Practice World, Unseen, and Enemy.

Maggie and Wheeler had exited also, remaining frozen on the new ground but observing the land in wonderment. They stood awestruck in the middle of a tall evergreen forest.

The railroad continued past where the train had stopped—no more than a single track. Harrison looked but could find no landmark, station, or anything extraordinary about where it had come to rest. His eyes stayed stuck on the ground. It was difficult to walk here for the land parallel to the rails was marked by deep impressions, as if a herd of stallions used the plot for their thoroughfare—a racetrack with no finish line.

The other Laochs were filing away from the tracks, into the forest, following some unmarked trail. Aubrey suggested they go out this way as well.

Harrison and Wheeler were in their element: a pathless trek through a wild wood. *Wild* being the perfect description. Except for the train tracks, this wilderness was untouched by anything manmade or even remotely human. It exuded a perceptible ancient quality, all the while wearing a newness about it. Rugged, but unmarred. Timeless, but also fresh.

Maggie caught up to Harrison and stuck by his side. Although she was intently watching her feet, he felt that she wanted to talk, so he paused to help her over a low branch across the way. They were the last in the line of hikers.

Hesitantly she spoke. "I want a chance to explain

myself."

Knowing that any explanation of hers would be long and exaggerated, he hastily let her off the hook. "Don't worry. I don't want to hear it."

"Please give me a chance," she implored pitifully.

"I don't care, Maggie. It's okay."

"But you think I'm a thief and a liar."

"So?" he spat. The force of his voice surprised him, as he felt no ill will toward her at that moment. He was always so cruel to her, even when he didn't mean to be. He hated that about himself but still blamed her for it.

"I didn't steal the knife, Harrison."

"I'm not listening." Not pausing to consider how childish he sounded, he picked up the pace to close the distance to Aubrey and Wheeler.

"He. Gave. It. To. Me," she added desperately, emphasizing each word.

Harrison barely noted her explanation.

"It's fine, Maggie. Just leave it alone." He was like his father in that way. He didn't care for excuses. What's done is done. It was best to move on.

Maggie grabbed his hand before he could leave her, but he shouted over his shoulder.

"Look, I don't want to hear it, okay? I'm feeling kind of great right now, and you're killing my buzz!"

"Harrison," she whispered.

The softness of her voice grabbed his attention, and he heard the quiet undercurrent of alarm. He glanced at her then and saw she wasn't looking at him but beyond. Fifteen feet from where they stood, something dark and enormous was spying on them.

It was a black bear on its fours. Another stood back a bit on its flanks. The latter bear's muscles could be seen slightly quivering under its fur. It was a testimony of power and presence . . . and danger.

A certain wisdom and amusement was evident in the bear's eyes. Its expression was very much like the coyote that had led the pack in the Crossing—wild and kind. And something else was there, too.

It was adoration.

Although the girl had her hand in his, it felt like a private experience for Harrison. He knew this was an important meeting.

Adrenaline ran its course through his body—his heart sputtered every half-minute and flew during the seconds in between. His senses were heightened as he waited to see if the bears would make a move. Aubrey and the other Laochs hadn't stopped, and this was, after all, a wild wood. Harrison didn't want a repeat of the chase for the train earlier that evening.

But the larger bear merely breathed at them. It turned its head as if to gesture to the retreating hiking party.

"I think we should . . . keep walking," Harrison suggested to Maggie in a shaky voice. "Slowly," he amended.

They left the bears and tread deliberately on shaky legs to join the rest of the company. They were quiet for a long while and frequently looked back over their shoulders to see if the animals would reappear.

"Thank you, Harrison," Maggie said gently, "for saving me from falling off the train."

"I didn't save you," he answered dejectedly.

"You reached for me," she corrected. "Thank you."

He yielded. "No problem."

16. THE MEADOW

From the patient and often-indulgent looks they were getting from the giants, Harrison figured that these mythical beings were used to a much faster pace. They might fly for all he knew. Many of them had gone on ahead, but three were left to suffer at the human rate of walking. Oddly, they seemed more than content to stay with them. Conversation was effortless and, when necessary, the silence was comfortable and not rushed.

Wheeler's companion was Juda, a smiley Middle-Eastern-looking fellow, who was clearly enjoying his cowboy threads. He kept quoting John Wayne and shooting imaginary things in the forest with his index finger. Wheeler fell right in with his humor, and the two brilliantly played off each other. The rest couldn't help but laugh.

"Young fella, if you're lookin' for trouble, I'll accommodate ya," Juda drawled.

Without missing a beat, Wheeler replied, "You do, and it'll be the biggest mistake you ever made, you Texas brushpopper!"

Maggie was doted on by Calista, who intimidated Harrison to no end. Although she was very friendly, Calista was so fiercely beautiful and tall that he couldn't get the lump out of his throat when she was near. She wore a long duster, which from the back made her appear to float ghost-like through the forest. The long white-blonde hair that streamed between her shoulder blades added to that illusion. Maggie seemed at ease with her at least.

The girl had more trouble with the terrain than the rest, because she was wearing a skirt and incompatible shoes. Harrison was ready to help her when needed, but Calista always got to her first.

The day had not advanced since they emerged from the tunnel. The sun was still setting . . . but not setting. It didn't move from its low position in the sky. It was twilight halted.

White and gold birds swept down from the branches, singing to the travelers. They dipped and swerved, like mid-air swimmers in a leafy reef.

After about an hour of navigating the woods, the forest changed, growing more colorful and less shadowy. Their feet began crunching over fallen leaves instead of soundless needles. The trees were multi-hued: yellows, reds, peaches, and plums. Flags of color joined the birds, swirling around their heads in a cool wind.

It was not the same season they had left in the Practice World. This was autumn. And the dying of The Highlands was sensational.

A clearing could be made out several yards ahead. And

music. . . .

"Leave your shoes here," Calista whispered, pointing to the edge of the wood. Harrison hadn't noticed that their otherworldly companions had sometime already shed their boots.

"Come along, partners," Aubrey instructed in his funny accent, "it is time we join the party."

The beating of drums welcomed them into the large meadow, wheat-colored and speckled with low blueberry bushes that had turned red for the season. It was indeed a party—a celebration to end the day of battle. The vibration of the music was felt beneath their bare feet and it thrummed all the way up into their chests, keeping time with their heartbeats.

Laochs played various stringed instruments: fiddles, mandolins, cellos, and unrecognized others. A band of pipes trilled on top, and the effect was an unexpected blend of Celtic and African tunes.

The beat had the distinct measure of train wheels clacking over the rails. It was a war song but also a love song. Harrison knew that without even thinking it through. The two themes mixed effortlessly—the violence of the drums emphasizing the romantic melody of the pipes and strings.

With her eyes closed, Calista was swaying to the music, rolling her shoulders. Her waterfall hair swung from side to side, and she silently spoke or sang or prayed in an unknown tongue. Harrison felt like a voyeur watching her, but it never occurred to him to look away.

THE HIGHLANDS TUNNEL

The others had changed from their dark clothing without veering from the western theme, so that they decorated the meadow with differing shades of green, blue, ivory, and red. Some danced, some chatted.

Other than the absurd perfection and height of the Laochs, the oddest thing about this ménage were the animals. Harrison catalogued the various species of mountain beasts: foxes, red and gray; bobcats; lots of deer, bucks and does with their fawns; black bears and coyotes—but these were not Harrison's friends from before, he observed. There were even several mountain lions. And smaller animals, too. Raccoons, squirrels, chipmunks, skunks, and birds.

They didn't keep to themselves either. The animals were quite sociable, and the giants looked to be enjoying their company. They didn't speak but they were definitely sharing something with one another.

Oh, and the food! After a while of enjoying the band, Aubrey steered them to long roughhewn log tables loaded with all sorts of sweets. They heaped pools of icing onto clay plates, into which they dipped fruits and sweet breads. Cakes, cookies, and pastries, too.

There was a large bowl of an unknown substance that Harrison could have sworn was Frosted Flakes in milk. Wheeler was eagerly ladling it into his mouth. Aware that Harrison was watching him stuff his face with disapproval, Wheeler turned to him, his cheeks full of the sugary food. Then he exaggeratedly rolled his eyes into his head while he chewed. "Mmmm," he hummed, until his older brother couldn't suppress his laughter anymore.

No matter how much they ate, they didn't feel too full. None of that sick, burdensome feeling from eating too many desserts. They felt as light and energetic as ever. And even better—they stayed hungry, so it seemed that when their eyes sighted more food, their stomachs growled for it.

It was every teenage boy's dream come true . . . well, other than maybe a multitude of beautiful girls. But there happened to be those, too, in the meadow. The female Laochs were breathtaking and very attentive. Wheeler was quite happy, although which he was more pleased about—the food or the women—no one could tell.

And speaking of females, Harrison found himself watching Maggie eat. He thought it endearing—the way she always took too much when it was available, to make up for a time in her early years when food wasn't as accessible.

The Highlands so far had been Harrison's own brand of adventure: cowboys, war, wild animals, a train ride, food, and music. Other than a few early glitches, it was perfect.

The boys asked the Laochs about their weapons, which they had left on the train, and how they fought in the war. Harrison knew Aubrey was an archer. But Aubrey explained grimly that most of the fighting was conducted without the use of weapons.

"What's your skill?" Wheeler asked Juda.

The easy-going giant was all too happy to demonstrate his talent with a staff. He picked up a long stick and started to spin and jab. Soon, however, his movements were a blur as he picked up speed and began to reel. Then his form came into focus and he sheepishly apologized for forgetting that the kids couldn't see what he was doing. He tried again in slow motion so that each action was distinct.

While the brothers were still applauding in amazement, the Laochs suddenly shifted and stood to attention, becoming as immobile as when they had stood in the train car the first time the three from Grant had seen them in the Crossing.

"It's time," Calista spoke.

The drums beat stronger until the sound seemed to fade and transform to the stomp of approaching hooves . . . louder . . . and louder . . . and louder.

Something was coming.

17. THE RIDER

A vigorous wind swept across the meadow, and all fell silent in the blast. Like water on the stovetop, murmurs streamed from the Laochs in breathy excitement. They looked at one another and grinned—the starry-eyed females held each other's arms. The musicians had stopped playing minutes ago, but the hoof beats took on a song of their own.

Here he comes.

This thought overtook all others in Harrison's head. The idea seized him by force—as though it hadn't really come from his mind at all.

What am I talking about? he asked himself, surprised. *I don't know who it is!*

Nevertheless, *he* was coming.

It's him, his thoughts persisted. *He—the . . . I don't know who, but it's Him.*

The whispering had reached a higher pitch, and Harrison was aware that somebody had started to sing. There were no words but a high trilling. Then another joined in . . . and another and another . . . until all the Laochs comprised an unearthly choir. Not one sang the same ballad, but they sang nonetheless, and it all blended melodically. The animals, too. It was euphoric. Even the ground came alive—the rocks, the trees. Every *thing* was singing.

Harrison looked at Wheeler, who grinned back at him, and then he turned his gaze back in the direction from which the galloping was heard—it was coming from the woods.

The anthem grew louder. It hurt his ears, but Harrison didn't mind. He wanted to shout along with them. Although the galloping sound became so loud that it seemed to come from all sides—from inside even—his eyes stayed focused on the point where the forest met the clearing.

And he came. On a black horse.

When the pair surfaced, Harrison was confused about whether he had been anticipating the horse or the man. Maybe both. Either way, it was him—the hero.

There were no words—and yet too many words—to describe them.

"It's him," Maggie said, voicing Harrison's conclusion. She sounded surer of who *he* was.

The Rider swung down from the horse's back and wrapped his arms around its neck, while it turned its head to rest on his shoulder. He was tall, but not like the Laochs. And he was handsome, but not like Aubrey—not perfect. It was a rugged beauty.

He was indeed a man! A human. Real, flesh and blood humanity. Like Harrison. His form didn't diminish the supernatural about him, however. He definitely possessed the magic . . . but he was from the Practice World, too, and that was comforting and intriguing.

The Rider turned away and let the partygoers tend to the horse, which they did with great ceremony and affection.

"Maggie," the man whispered with the ghost of a smile at the corner of his mouth.

Maggie shrieked and took off to meet him, bolting past the giants. She almost didn't make it. Once in his shadow, she started to collapse, but the Rider captured her in his arms and kissed her forehead before setting her back on her feet. Her eyes squeezed shut, as though she had been waiting for that kiss her whole life and didn't want it to be over so soon.

Gripping her arms, he spoke to her with such gentleness and sincerity that Harrison felt his face flush.

"What am I going to do with you, *chica?* Hmmm?" He looked at her adoringly, clearly savoring the moment as much as Maggie.

"Do you want to meet him?" Juda asked.

Wheeler nodded eagerly.

Harrison's breath caught in his throat when he realized that the man was making his way through the crowd toward them. With an arm around Maggie's shoulders, the Rider grinned and walked toward the brothers. Harrison saw that the girl's face was wet with tears.

The Rider wore a blue collared shirt with a gray pinstriped, buttoned vest but no boots—his feet were bare, like all the others. His look mixed the cowboy with piratical details. His hair was longish, and it stuck out from under a colonial tricorn hat. He sported a growth of stubble on his face and leather bands that tied around his wrists.

"Wheeler. Harrison." He smiled and looked at each boy in turn. His eyes were a silvery gray-brown. Like the last fallen leaf of autumn, with a smudge of its former green.

"Do I know you?" Harrison asked.

"*Do* you know me?" he turned the question on him.

"I think so, yeah."

He nodded, enthusiastic for being recognized. "You can call me Brother."

18. MAGGIE'S HERO

If Brother and his horse were the hosts of The Highlands, Maggie, Harrison, and Wheeler were the guests of honor.

Being with Brother that evening churned a mixture of emotion within Harrison. He felt totally shaken and, for the first time in a long time, put together. He wanted Brother's attention, but if he allowed himself to think too much about it, he felt rather exposed in Brother's sight. As if Brother were well acquainted with Harrison's dark side. There was no evidence of that—it was just a feeling, like Brother could tell him all his secrets. And if he were privy, he didn't let on or allow it to get in the way of their conversation.

A cropping of rocks divided the meadow, and Brother reclined in the dent of one large boulder with his hat on his knee. A group of turtles, like clunky animated rocks themselves, shared the seating with the humans and listened.

The horse attended, too. Its presence was large—felt all around—but comforting. Its rumblings and nods surrounded the guests, and it chewed repeatedly on Wheeler's shirt sleeve, making him giggle. Brother met its eyes consistently as he spoke. Harrison had the peculiar urge to fling himself on its back, grab onto its mane, and ride the craggy, enchanted territory of The Highlands. The horse gazed at him meaningfully, as if in response to his unspoken desires—like it wanted that, too.

Maggie was pressed into Brother's side, and he bridged one bent leg possessively over her body. This posture would have been considered inappropriate in the Practice World, but it didn't concern anybody here, much less Maggie. The vulnerability she had hidden all afternoon had leaked and it now showed on her face. The fear from being accused and chased, the anger . . . and the relief of being held by Brother.

She leaned into him, brow furrowed, and spoke quietly but earnestly in Spanish. From her petulant expression and teary eyes, Harrison guessed that she was complaining, and he wondered nervously if it was about him. Brother listened seriously, nodding and stroking her head. Finally, one big tear escaped and began to roll down her face, before Brother wiped it away. After that, Maggie's grievance, whatever it had been about, seemed to be expunged.

Although she may have been "telling" on him, Harrison also sensed a burden lift once Brother had showed up. He didn't have to be the hero anymore; he could lay off and Maggie and Wheeler would be okay.

The four of them relaxed into equal parts of conversation and silence. It didn't matter whom Brother addressed, to Harrison, it felt as if all Brother's attention were focused on him. He felt recognized . . . he felt *chosen.*

The man was just so cool! Harrison thought distractedly that Maggie must prefer the roguishly handsome, kind of bad-boy type. He wondered how he could alter his own appearance to imitate it . . . maybe do something different with his hair gel.

And yet he still didn't know who Brother was. He was definitely older than a real big brother would be, but there was also something very youthful and sort of rebellious about him.

"I hope the walk here wasn't bad. Aubrey's sensitive, but sometimes even he forgets our human limitations." Brother lifted a shoulder.

"Nah, it was okay," replied Wheeler.

"Oh! We saw a bear." Harrison met Brother's gaze. "Two bears, actually, but the one. . . ." He wasn't sure how to describe it.

"Right, well, that wasn't a real bear."

"Oh." Harrison said.

Maggie looked up at Brother, puzzled. Nobody thought to ask what *it* was if it wasn't a bear. Harrison jolted at a new realization: two bears, two hawks, two coyotes.

"The coyotes—friends of the bears maybe?" he asked.

"Now you're catching on." Brother chuckled. When he smiled, his mouth curled up farther on the one side, very much in the cowboy fashion. He certainly was charming Maggie. "Sorry about the coyotes, by the way. We didn't mean to frighten you. It's just that we needed you to catch the train. After Wheeler got on, you didn't have much of a choice about it."

"They chased us," Maggie accused. "We could have been hurt. I almost got bit!"

"You wouldn't have been hurt bad, *loca*." He pinched her chin. "You're used to running."

Maggie couldn't help the laugh that escaped. "Oh, Brother! You are no gentleman!" she chided with humor.

He shrugged apologetically and laughed with her. "Nope," he agreed mirthfully.

"He's the original gangster," Wheeler interjected.

"No, your man here wouldn't have let you get hurt." Brother indicated Harrison with a nod. The boy reflexively touched the scar under his eye and registered intense pride when Brother called him "your man."

"I'm not that good at running," he admitted.

"Yeah, he can't breathe through his nose. He could have suffocated," Wheeler reported.

"It's true," Harrison said seriously, but soon he was grinning sheepishly, and they all laughed for all the times they could have been hurt that day.

"I heard my name mentioned a moment ago." Aubrey approached the little gathering.

"Oh, I was just saying that sometimes you all are hard on us men," Brother answered.

"Never," countered Aubrey. "Well, perhaps a bit," he

conceded. "Ah, and speaking of you men—and young lady, of course—you three will be spending tomorrow with Brother."

"That's right," Brother took over. "So think about what you want to do. Let's see . . . it's fall now, then," he said looking up, "it will be winter tomorrow."

A wind blew in response to his statement and leaves fluttered from overhead like a ticker-tape parade. The humans raised eyebrows at each other.

"This is an excellent party," Wheeler said after a span of quiet.

"Wait 'til you see the party we throw when this war is over," Brother stated.

"Can we?"

"Sure, you'll be here. I promise. But I'm glad you could be here now. It's important." He dragged a hand down over his mouth and stroked his scratchy chin.

"Yeah, are you going to tell us what we're doing here?" Harrison asked.

"Can you wait until tomorrow?"

"I think so."

"Okay, then. Tomorrow," he vowed.

When Brother had ridden into the meadow, the sun finished its setting. A faint smile of a moon shone in the blue-gray sky. After an age, it was well dark and the Laochs built a bonfire. The smoke floated in the air around their heads, filtering through their hair and nostrils, but it was a surprisingly pleasant effect. That's when Harrison realized that he was breathing through

THE HIGHLANDS TUNNEL

his nose. He could smell the fire and the food: smoky and spicy. He smelled hay, too, and it didn't make him sneeze.

"Bonus!" Harrison whispered to himself. He could breathe in The Highlands.

19. THE RITE

The Laochs carried torches and moved to dance in a circle around the fire while the drums continued to pound out their endless rhythm. The ring of giants, interspersed with wild animals and birds, caused Harrison to recall the old stories. He, too, it seemed had stepped past the boundaries of the wardrobe, fallen down the rabbit hole, and flown out the nursery window on a cloud of pixie dust. It was no accident, though—he was made for this story, and it was meant for him.

Maybe it should have felt like a dream or a delusion, but strangely, his time in The Highlands seemed more real than his life at the farmhouse and in Grant altogether. He might give more to credit such fantasies in the future.

It was natural to accept . . . perhaps because of the legends and myths. Even if he couldn't interpret the Laoch language, he somehow understood what was being said. They had begun with a chant around the fire, and the chanting had turned into storytelling. Tales about the magic of The Highlands; the Ancient Ones, called the Laoch warriors; and the heart of The Highlands: the Giver. Also the Ransom. Harrison couldn't quite make out the details of the plot, but it was very old, and he caught the essence of it, especially when the battle scenes played like movie clips above the fire.

He remembered the story Aubrey had told him on the train. About the Unseen. There was an Enemy out there beyond tunnel, and it had threatened Harrison personally. He wasn't exactly sure what or who the Ransom was, but it had everything to do with the Great War that the Laochs fought.

Harrison didn't feel tired, but he couldn't stop yawning. Every other minute his mouth opened wide as if something wanted to escape him. Harrison considered instead that something wanted in. He didn't try to stifle it.

In the firelight, Brother's features changed. His previous gentle expression had alchemized into a fierce warrior's mask. His eyes displayed a haunted sorrow, too. His hair looked to be ablaze, dancing in the fire, and he was all at once an extension of the fire. Harrison was suddenly aware of strange markings on Brother's body—scars running up and down his arms and neck—adding to his outlaw persona. This man had been in the battle, too.

Harrison shifted his sight to Maggie, who sat next to Brother. In the fire-lit evening, her eyes stayed closed. Her head was no doubt filled with the otherworldly language of the stories. The residual little-girl qualities were refined in the light, turning sharp and tribal. High cheekbones that made her lidded eyes to disappear in the shadows. That was until she opened them. Then two small points of black liquid light glared point-blank at Harrison. She was powerful and wild-looking, like an Indian princess at a war party. This was no damsel in distress; she was a blazing member of the mission.

It occurred to him that the ritual had changed them all . . . except, of course, for those who do not change—the Laochs. Harrison turned his head sharply to view Wheeler. He was still a boy, but definitely something more now. The impish, untamed Wheeler was not replaced . . . but honed. He was raw, ready, primal.

Harrison wished he could see his own person, a reflection of how his tousled self had changed in the light of the campfire. But a vise of humiliation snatched that thought. What if the removal of his mask would reveal something dark or base? Some flaw or weakness he didn't want Brother to see—or Maggie, for that matter. How many times had he played the bad guy? It came all too easy for Harrison. He self-consciously wiped a palm over his face.

The storytelling morphed into a soft and everlasting song. And atop the low singing, Brother spoke. Actually, it was rather like shouting. His brown-green eyes glowed passionate as he issued declarations in the Highland tongue. The Laochs, when not singing, repeated certain phrases and called out their contributions. The fire responded to his foreign rant, too, by rising and sparking.

Then Harrison heard Brother say his name—but it wasn't his birth name. It was another. And although he wasn't sure why he thought he was being referenced, he knew he was being called, because when he heard the name it felt as though his insides had burst out of his body and run to Brother without the rest of him. It was the most wonderful word he had ever heard, and he so craved to hear it again, for it resonated with something within him. Brother met his gaze, and Harrison walked to him.

Brother held the knife—it was Maggie's stolen weapon—he recognized the markings. Harrison wasn't sure what was going to happen next. Brother might hurt him, but he didn't care. He trusted enough to go along with the order of service. Instead of cutting, Brother held it out to the boy on open hands—one on the blade, the other on the handle. The sheath was missing.

Then the horse trotted over, speaking to Harrison.

"It's your choice, Harrison. I've already chosen you, but you must follow me if this is what you want."

It took a moment for it to register in his mind that the horse had spoken to him. Not audibly, as one would expect, but even so, it had talked.

It needn't have asked. Although he appreciated the opportunity to decline, Harrison wanted more than anything to accept. There was no more choice involved.

He received the knife from Brother and a loud

shout of approval rose up from the Highlanders. Harrison looked to Brother, the master of ceremonies, and inferred from the honored expression returning his that he was to fight in the war now. This unconventional knighting ceremony was the hero inviting him to be a character in his story.

When Harrison lifted the knife above his head to signal his acceptance, the shouts grew even more raucous, so that their chorus filled his head and he yawned once again.

THE HIGHLANDS TUNNEL

20. CAMPING

The dream ended abruptly with a blaze of fire. Harrison had been chasing the Unseen Enemy, which was—aptly so—unseen. The hawks, on the other hand, ever-present and circling his head, had shrieked with fear as he lunged at them with his knife. Then he saw Brother's face suddenly in front of his and it all went up in smoke.

Then he dreamed he was flying. Or perhaps he was falling. Whichever it was, it was sublime.

At some point earlier in the evening, Aubrey had arranged tents to be set up for the humans. Apparently, the Laochs didn't sleep; or if they did, they preferred to do it without a ceiling. Harrison didn't recall leaving the party, which continued on into the wee hours, but he woke up sometime in the middle of the night when Brother roused him.

"Harrison, are you awake?"

"Mmm-hmm," he sort of agreed, coming out of his flying-falling dream.

"I'm sorry to disturb you, but I couldn't let this go without waking you."

"S'okay. What is it?" Harrison was actually thrilled to be sharing a midnight spell with Brother and was eager to know what it was he needed. He tried to act casual as he waited for Brother to explain, but he was fighting the urge to jump up and run a lap around the tent.

"C'mon. I want to show you something."

Harrison grabbed his blanket and followed Brother out of the tent, passing Wheeler's slumbering form. Once outside, he wrapped the blanket around his shoulders. He'd left his shoes at the edge of the wood, but his naked feet didn't cause him discomfort.

Maggie was sharing the adjacent tent with Calista, who offered to stay the night with her. Harrison wanted to look in, but he wasn't sure it was appropriate—it certainly went against his mother's version of propriety. He still had to get used to the idea that he wouldn't be scolded here. These "people" looked like adults, after all. But so far the Laochs had been very accommodating.

After a short deliberation, he figured it was okay to check on Maggie.

"She's fine," Calista said with a smile when he poked his head into the tent for a peek. "She's dreaming."

Calista—who was stroking a rabbit that dozed on her lap—looked approving of Harrison's gallantry. *Huh*, he thought, *so the Ancient Ones don't sleep*. He wondered where his buddy Aubrey was hanging out.

Maggie was indeed dreaming, her long dark hair

splayed out over the bedding. A wind invaded through the flap Harrison held up, and it caused strands of her hair to dance on the pillow like aisles of narrow waves on an onyx ocean. Seeing her slight body inert under the blanket wakened this protective nature he'd recently recognized—although she was obviously well guarded. Again, he was baffled that such a girl could irritate him so terribly one moment, only to make him feel bound to her the next!

Harrison returned Calista's smile and ducked out, securing the opening against the nighttime air. When he turned around, Brother was gone. He took a few steps into the meadow.

"I'm here," Brother said from behind.

"Oh." Harrison twisted to face him.

"Look!" He pointed at the night sky above the tents, making big gestures at the stars. "Let's go up farther. I know a trail."

The two hiked through the dark, not talking. Brother's silence reminded Harrison of his horse, who had chosen to communicate telepathically when the time came during the fire ceremony. When that had happened, Harrison became aware that the horse had been trying to speak to him all evening, but it was only by the fire that the boy finally grasped the power to understand.

The trail led steeply up and took less than ten minutes to reach the top. Harrison concentrated on the dirt path beneath his feet, so he wouldn't stumble in the darkness. The end of the trail was a narrow cliff that overlooked the forest surrounding the meadow. Harrison and Brother lay on their backs on the flat rock precipice and watched the sky.

Judging by a hurried glance, it didn't seem any more extraordinary than a night skyscape in the Practice World. The canvas was indigo blue and the moon, which had been a slight crescent earlier that evening, was now full and white.

A rumbling from the nearby cover of trees announced another guest that would join their sky-gazing party. Heavy padded footsteps came nearer until the visitor was at Harrison's back, breathing loudly. It flattened itself to the ground in one thunderous descent, so that its warm, fur-covered body matched itself exactly to Harrison's. It sighed contentedly once arranged comfortably on the rock.

Harrison didn't need to look, because he knew it was one of the black bears he and Maggie had encountered that evening in the forest—not a real bear, Brother had said. He rolled closer to this oversized, living teddy, finding pleasure in its resonating sighs and satisfied growls.

But it was the stars from which Harrison could not take his eyes away. They moved. Like a dance . . . and not a ballet, either. It was a pulsing, quick rhythm the stars leapt and twirled to, but he was not able to hear it. He imagined it was something like the earth-thumping meadow music, except that this symphony was celestial.

The stars seemed so close that he only had to reach

up from where he was lying to touch one. More than a symbol or metaphor, these were his dreams from the Practice World. He held so many hopes and desires and potential adventures up in the air like that, winking and teasing and skittering about just above his head. Because he could simply snatch any one with his fingers and pull it to himself, he was at peace. Knowing the dream was attainable made it okay, whether it was realized or not.

    He didn't need to go back to the Practice World; he wanted to stay in The Highlands. He decided he would talk to Brother about it the next day—about how to get Wheeler and Maggie back without him.

THE HIGHLANDS TUNNEL

21. WINTER

Morning arrived with a refreshing chill. Harrison and Wheeler woke up in their sleeping bags, although Harrison didn't remember going back to the tent after his midnight hike with Brother.

Wheeler opened the flaps of the shelter and peered out.

"Yep, it's winter."

"Really?" Harrison asked, but he wasn't skeptical.

Wheeler nodded. "There's snow and everything."

"Okay. So what do you want to do with Brother today?"

"I don't know for sure. What about you? Have you thought about it?"

Harrison shrugged. He had thought a lot about it actually. The anticipation of spending time with Brother—activity being open to whim—was very appealing. Since his sinuses had opened, running was an option. Running fast and free, testing his abilities in this new enhanced environment. But no. He had run quite enough the day before—that idea didn't tempt him at all.

THE HIGHLANDS TUNNEL

Everything seemed possible in The Highlands, so naturally, Harrison's first desire would be a common one: flying. He flew often in his dreams, and he wondered if he could fly here. Some instinct told him that yes, indeed he could fly.

As grand a vision as it made, he was intimidated. But not for fear of his safety. He would need instruction, fairy dust, or whatever. The thought of having to be held or tutored really turned him off. As much as he wanted to fly—he could feel the sensation even as he imagined it—he knew it wasn't his time yet. Since he had this opportunity, he wanted to show Brother what he could do already. Some talent or skill that would impress his host.

"Brother really is great, isn't he?" Harrison said aloud.

"Yeah, but he makes me hungry," Wheeler complained. "Do you think those giants have got breakfast ready yet?"

"Well, let's go see."

They shrugged into their jackets and departed their makeshift bedroom. Harrison felt the weight of the knife against his side in his sweater pocket.

The trouble was, the boys could not find the Laochs. Besides Maggie and their tents, the meadow was unpopulated.

"They don't seem like the slacker types, but maybe they slept in," Wheeler speculated.

"How did you sleep, Maggie?" Harrison asked. He sometimes hesitated to offer her questions, because it provided the opportunity to answer, and her responses could carry on for a long while. But he was feeling charitable this morning and really wanted to hear.

She looked past him, enraptured. "Fine, thanks. I woke up in the night. I saw this ball of light in my tent, hovering right above my face. I was half asleep still, so I just smiled and said to myself, 'That's nice—a fairy.'"

Wheeler snickered.

"A fairy? Really?" Harrison questioned.

"I don't think it was really a fairy . . . but it was *something*," Maggie explained. "I mean, isn't it strange that we just accept everything that's going on here? I wasn't even surprised to wake up to a ball of floating light glowing in my face—fairy or whatever it was."

"Or to wake up to snow," Wheeler stated, surreptitiously tossing a snowball in his brother's hair.

He knew from experience that he didn't mess with Harrison's hair without it resulting in a fight. Therefore a brief but good-natured tussle ensued as Harrison caught Wheeler in a headlock and shoved his face into a snow drift. It was cold but not wet. Maggie laughed but made a stern motion so the boys understood they would be sorry if they tried to involve her.

"Maybe they brainwashed us, or there was something in the food. . . ." Wheeler suggested when Harrison let up. "We could be tripping."

"Or maybe we died," Maggie said flippantly.

"All three of us at once," Harrison said incredulously. "How?"

THE HIGHLANDS TUNNEL

"Of fright!"

"So was that it?" Harrison asked, dusting flakes from his head. "You didn't see . . . the fairy again?"

"No. I closed my eyes and a moment later, Brother woke me up. You know . . . where is Brother?" Maggie questioned. "We're supposed to spend today with him."

"Brother woke me up last night, too," Wheeler said to Harrison.

That reminded him. "Uh, speaking of that . . . Maggie, yesterday you obviously recognized Brother when you saw him. Who is he?"

"Oh. . . ." She was at a loss for words. "He's . . . you know—he's . . . the hero."

"That's what I thought," Harrison murmured, bemused *and* enlightened.

The horse sauntered into the clearing, kicking up snow as it came, and stood with the humans. In the bright winter sun, they could detect a disguised brindled pattern in the horse's coat. It snorted a friendly greeting and hung its head between them. Maggie rested her cheek against its shoulder.

"Brother's here. I can feel him," Harrison said suddenly. "I'll go find him." He trudged off hastily into the woods in the direction he felt pulled, which looked black a few trees in from where they'd stood in the field.

Harrison was hoping to catch Brother alone. He felt somewhat jealous that he wasn't the only one who had spent some of the night with the Rider. There was a lot he wanted to know.

Once he made it to the first row of trees, the shadows opened up and he saw Brother leaning against a tree, hands in pockets, watching him approach. All Harrison's anxiousness dissolved.

"Hey." Brother's lips curved into a grin.

"Hey." Harrison paused. "Where's Aubrey and the rest?"

"They took the train back to the Practice World."

"Okay." *Good.* Harrison was glad he wasn't made to get on the morning train. He could stay in The Highlands . . . for now.

All of a sudden he did a double take, staring in shock at Brother's face, which had changed.

"Don't be afraid," he quickly reassured. "It's just my eyes that change—nothing else."

"I wasn't afraid," Harrison insisted.

"I know."

Brother's eyes had turned blue.

"What do you want to do?" Brother asked.

"Uh . . . well, shouldn't we go get the other two?"

"Don't worry. They're not alone, and we'll catch up with them later."

"The horse. Right. Okay." Was he supposed to feel guilty for not even telling them where he was going? Perhaps, but he didn't hesitate to follow. He trusted that Brother would not leave Maggie and Wheeler in the meadow unless they would be entertained.

"What do you want to do?" Brother repeated.

"Well. . . ." Harrison mentally listed all the things he could accomplish confidently, then he selected a relevant one. "We could go climbing, maybe? Since we're in the mountains, I mean."

"Brilliant. I thought you might want to climb." Brother's back bounced away from the tree trunk and he bent to retrieve a backpack that was resting near his bare feet, which were buried in the snow. He still sported the anachronistic costume. "Follow me."

He reached into the pack and pulled out some torn bread and a pear and handed it back to Harrison.

"Here. Breakfast on the road."

22. REBELS

After walking for a distance—odd, but it seemed to Harrison that they were trekking downhill to go climbing—they emerged from the woods beside a snow-banked stream, not frozen, but rushing with swollen urgency over boulders and logs. Harrison noticed the crisp smell of snow and sharp evergreen. Brother stopped and took two bottles from his pack.

"We ought to fill these to take with us. You know what they say about altitude and dehydration. . . ."

As he knelt with the bottle Brother had handed him, Harrison muttered sarcastically, "Yeah, I know what *they* say."

Brother picked up on the implication and smiled. Harrison always reacted bitterly to any rule . . . even if it were for his own good.

"I think you might have a problem with authority, young man," Brother joked, teeth gleaming like the snow.

"Hey, I follow the rules," he insisted.

"Yeah, but you resent them. Why?"

Harrison took a swallow of the icy water. "I don't

know. I just don't like being told what to do."

"I think it's because you've been made to be something you're not."

"Hmmm. Maybe."

Wasn't that the truth, though? His inner turbulence had made the adults uncomfortable and untrusting. Wheeler was the rowdy one. That was looked down on by most adults, but at least it was understood and somewhat expected. Harrison was dark on the inside. Stormy. He possessed a ferocious appetite for information and a temper. He usually chose to resist his natural urges to save himself the trouble . . . and judgment.

"Wow, this water is good. And what about you? No offense, but you look to be something of a rebel." Harrison wanted to know more about Brother. He wore a mischievous expression most of the time.

"Me? I always think of a smart thing to say at times when it's not smart—and even dangerous—to say it. It takes a lot of self-control. I certainly can make the authorities mad on occasion, even when I'm not trying to," he answered wistfully.

Harrison smiled, entertained. He was quite aware he was speaking to an authority figure, even if Brother was a rebel. Power radiated from his posture and voice, but he managed it in a humble, comfortable sort of way.

"That's just it, isn't it? It seems that grown-ups will think what they want without asking you how you feel or what your intentions are." Brother was—technically speaking—a "grown-up," but it also registered in Harrison's mind that Brother was something else entirely. Ghosts couldn't really be considered part of the grown-up crowd, could they?

He continued. "Be on time, be polite, get good grades, don't complain. If you get into trouble, you're a bad kid. They don't want to hear about any crazy ideas or feelings that don't make any sense."

"You're mostly right. I do remember that well. And Wheeler probably feels the same. And Maggie," Brother responded softly.

Oh, Maggie.

Accused of stealing, Harrison had charged her with guilt even before he'd found the knife on her. All the more, he wouldn't let her explain. That knife, now in his own pocket, suddenly weighed a lot more. It had become his burden.

Harrison was amused—if slightly chagrined—to discover he had been rebuked. It had been so gentle and indirect that he couldn't feel ashamed or irritated, but anxious to make it right. He must get the chance to change for her. To make her want him.

It was in that moment that Harrison realized he had let his guard down. He didn't have to act rebuffed or apologetic. Brother knew all his secrets anyway. He smiled ruefully.

"Yeah, I guess I was acting just like my dad, huh?"

"Well . . . it's understandable. Besides, your dad's not so bad."

That comment opened up a well of emotion for

Harrison. He was talking to Brother like he would his friend Luke.

"I know. I've seen plenty worse. He just doesn't want to know me." He continued, imitating his father's voice and sighing heavily, " 'After-school detention for a week, huh? Okay, where's the slip I'm supposed to sign.' That's it. He doesn't yell or lecture—that's my mom's specialty—or even get angry. And I'm glad of that, but . . . when the trouble with the law happened, we grew apart." The memory of the barn burning was an unwelcome one, so he pushed it under and went on. "He stopped spending time with me, talking to me, touching me, too. It was like we didn't know how to be with each other anymore." He scowled. "I don't want to think about the trouble that's waiting for me after all this . . . back home."

Brother's reply was quiet. "Cort grew up without his father, you know. He doesn't know how to be what you need. He loves you so much, he's afraid he's going to make a mistake or be a bad influence for you. Of course, he's already hurt you with his distance. And your mother, despite her good intentions, struggles with her own broken heart. She doesn't approve of your father's . . . wildness." Harrison's brow wrinkled. "Yes, he's got it, too. She's tamed him, though, in ways your grandmother couldn't. Aye. . . ." he uttered like a curse.

Harrison guessed, "So, you're saying that they do the best they can, right?"

"Right. But it isn't enough. . . . See sometimes the

people you think are the safest actually pose the greatest threat." Brother spoke to the evergreen boughs above his head.

"My mother, for instance," he continued with a small smile, "always wanted me to perform for people. She was a wonderful mother; she loved so strongly, but Crikey Moses, was that woman maddening sometimes!" They laughed and Brother's voice softened. "Mothers can be lovely, though. Mothers teach us to pour a glass and not to drink straight out of the milk carton. They show us barbarians how to live civilly in the Practice World, but they also give us a peek at what's beyond." He ended with something that looked like reverence winking in his eyes.

Acknowledging their weaknesses, Harrison thought of his own parents with fondness and compassion. His mother—who offered him a certain regard that he knew would always be available no matter what—loved him and relied on him. As for his father . . . well, he felt it in reverse. That no matter what, he would always respect his father and crave his company and approval. He thought of his teachers next, Mr. Kelly and Ms. Knight. His stomach performed a flip that rivaled Ringling Brothers when he remembered his physics teacher, and yet he chose not to dwell on that.

"So my dad was trouble, too," Harrison prompted. "Oh, you should've seen him when he was younger. He was a lot like Wheeler—always into some mischief. The fireworks in the barn were a fitting tribute to your father and his youth. A lot of fun Cort Bentley was. I'm surprised the nation's capital stood standing with that rascal growing up there. Actually, it probably surprised your grandmother that he lived to grow up at all."

"My dad? Really? Is that why my *grand-mere* always looks so suspicious?"

"Mm-hm. That mischievous energy . . . believe it or not, I can use that. You, however, are actually more like your grandfather."

"Th—the one I'm named for?" The coward.

"Yes. Very curious, intelligent, but very private. Always plotting and often slipping under the radar. Quite the rebel."

Harrison couldn't say anything to that. His heart beat quick but heavy.

"You know, this thing in you that you've been trying so hard to cure? It's the very thing you were made for." Brother held his focus. "If you think I esteem you because you've learned to restrict it and be what your parents want you to be, you're wrong. I'm fond of you for who you are."

"And what is that?" Harrison really didn't know.

"You'll have to discover it again for yourself. Once you stop acting on that innate, inside voice, it becomes more and more buried, harder to hear. It's like drinking cold hot chocolate. There's a better way, only you've become so used to experiencing life as it is. But you can emerge from the tunnel . . . eventually."

Harrison wanted very much to know who he was

and his purpose. He thought of the bonfire and what he had come to think of as his naming ceremony. He was chosen, but was he brave enough to see it through without bailing?

"Are we going to climb that?" Harrison pointed to the mass of gray snow-covered rock hovering before them.

"Yeah," Brother nodded, eyes wide and lips pressed into a long smile.

"Cool. Let's get going," Harrison said, gazing at the mountain. Until now, the landscape had mirrored the Virginia Blue Ridge, but this looked like the Great Rocky Mountains of the West.

"Okay. Wait, though—I brought your shoes. Thought we might need 'em." Brother pulled out two pairs of cowboy boots and handed one to Harrison, who had been expecting to see his checkered Vans, which were left at the edge of the meadow.

"Oh, these aren't mine."

"They'll fit," Brother assured.

Harrison inspected them suspiciously, flexing the soles and squeezing the toes. He didn't think cowboy boots would be very comfortable footwear for the activity they had in mind.

"What are you doing?" Brother watched the boot examination quizzically.

"Well, you know what *they say* about snakes in your boots."

Brother was shaking with laughter. "First of all, you smart alec, there's six inches of snow on the ground, and second, there are no snakes in The Highlands."

"Figures," Harrison responded good-naturedly.

23. THE CLIMB

He had to admit, the boots did actually feel good.

The climb was gradual at first—it was not even necessary to hold on—but then the boulders made their debut and eventually advanced to sheer rock faces. Harrison was quite an expert at it, and he enjoyed the adrenaline that rushed his system when he looked down and saw how far he'd already come. Although he had no difficulty himself, Brother readily admitted how impressed he was with his companion's skill.

Did it make it easier knowing that nothing bad could happen here? That was Harrison's theory anyway. He was fairly certain that accidents didn't happen in The Highlands. This was a land in which you ate desserts with bears and camped out with fairies. And the Unseen Enemy, which he hadn't even known existed before he'd arrived here, was not allowed on the premises. That was not to say he wasn't afraid. There was snow and ice on the rocks, and he slipped frequently. And it would be a long drop if he fell. But the fear was part of the amusement.

Brother was deliberate about not touching, being

careful not to try to catch Harrison when he lost his footing. It was a demanding process. Typically the danger would be the draw of the climb, but here, it was pure challenge! Was he stubborn enough to reach the top?

At one point during the climb, they had to jump over a ravine. For all the boy knew, the crack ran the whole of the mountain down to flat ground—that was, if it had an end. Peering into its black depths, Harrison remembered jumping the gaps between traveling train cars in the night. The memory made him uneasy.

The Crossing. It was much like that ravine. Harrison didn't belong in the divide . . . but on which side was home? During the time spent in the Crossing, he was more afraid of what awaited him beyond the tunnel. Now that he was here, he felt more unsettled about the Practice World . . . or he would have had he thought much about it.

Throughout the endeavor, especially during the handful of straightforward sections on the trail, Brother listened to Harrison tell him jokes and stories in response to his careful questions. He had this appealing way of making the conversation all about Harrison. Then, after doubling over with laughter at Harrison's perfected—if exaggerated—mimicry of his very proper and busybody neighbor Mrs. Dunbar, Brother threw out a non-sequitur, changing the rhythm of the exchange.

"You used to love trains."

"Yeah, well my dad's into trains, you know. I helped

him with his railroad model in the cellar."

"Why do you think your dad likes trains so much?"

This new discussion was meant to reveal something. Harrison figured that, because Brother hadn't asked such a question before. It seemed that he was ready to give a teaching. Harrison supposed it would be interesting, so he played along.

"Trains are big . . . powerful . . . manmade machines."

"That's part of it . . . but there's more," Brother encouraged.

"Because they work really hard," he guessed again.

"No." Brother indicated with his hand that Harrison should try again.

"Because they're fast, strong. . . ." His answer sounded more like a question.

Brother shook his head and laughed through his nose.

Harrison was slightly exasperated and rolled his eyes . . . but it may have been the altitude getting to him. "I don't know—because they're usually on time." He was being cheeky, but Brother just laughed.

"Why's that funny?" Harrison retorted, not *very* angry.

"It's your answers. They're so telling." He wiped his hand over his mouth and chin. "Oh, Harrison! I'm so happy you're here. Are those the reasons why people like you, do you think? Because you're smart, tall, good-looking, talented, and dependable?" He grinned at him.

THE HIGHLANDS TUNNEL

Harrison didn't answer because frankly, yes, those were the sorts of honorable, useful characteristics that earned him regard.

Brother continued. "No. For your dad, it's the symbolism. Journey, romance, adventure, transport."

Harrison thought about it. Yes, he suspected that a long time ago he valued trains for those reasons.

"I didn't choose you because you're responsible or because you've learned to tame or overcome your wild self. I didn't bring you here because you know how to behave. I want you because you're you. Trains are meant to stay on tracks, not people."

Harrison's brain skipped right over the direct message about his behavior and clutched onto the "I want you" bit. Brother wanted him. Harrsion wanted to shout, *I want you, too!* He was greedy; he wanted all of it, Brother and The Highlands . . . forever.

The Highlands was his homeland, his country. There were no limits here. It was definitely worth the jump and whatever risks they gambled to make it through the tunnel. As unnerving as it was to leave the boundaries that made him feel safe and normal in the Practice World, once he did, the release was exhilarating. That was freedom, and Harrison did not want to give it up!

The closer they got to the summit, however, the more something troubled him. He intuited that Brother was preparing him to go back. It was like this whole excursion was designed to show Harrison that he had what it took to face the trouble at home.

He was confused, though. Why had he been given the knife? What did it mean to be chosen? And . . . oh! How could he leave here? The wild lands open for exploration and discovery. Aubrey and the other Laochs. The horse—in a way that surprised him—he wanted so desperately to ride with the horse. The perpetual music. The perpetual silence. How could he leave Brother? It panicked him to think about it. Didn't Brother know that he would follow him anywhere? But Wheeler . . . and Maggie. How could he let them go?

It was time for answers. He wanted to know what he was doing here. Brother hadn't explained anything yet, so Harrison supposed he was to initiate the interrogation. He would wait until they reached the top, and then Brother must tell all.

Harrison glided his hands across a moss-covered rock by his face that was iced over. He let the warmth of his body melt the glaze that encased the feathery green plant until he finally felt its soft chilled texture. When he pressed farther, his hand met immovable rock. He grabbed it and used his hold to lift his body onto the flat top of it. Brother remained several yards below Harrison's ledge, clinging to the side of the cliff. Sizing up this newly achieved level, Harrison saw a great pine tree looming before him and a dirt path beside it.

He'd reached the top.

An imposing bald eagle was perched on a low branch of the pine, and it watched Harrison with wise yellow eyes. The boy got to his feet and walked to the tree and met the bird. It looked so benevolent and peaceful that he didn't think to associate it with his recent winged tormentors in the Crossing.

"Where's the other eagle, mate?" he asked it. The other animals had come in pairs. But then he remembered there was only the one horse—and one bear in the night.

It looked at him much the way the bear had . . . and the horse and the coyote. It was centered on Harrison and a meaningful connection passed between them. The eagle spread its wings wide. Harrison experienced an intense need saturating his insides and rushing straight to his feet, which carried him to the bird, who wrapped him in a feathered embrace.

It loved him. It adored him! It needed him. *Why?* he wondered. Because he had reached the top? Harrison didn't know, but he soaked it up.

When it let go, he wiped his face and followed the path to the inevitable precipice. When he saw the view that welcomed him he gasped and then smiled. He stepped to the edge of the cliff and basked in the reward of the climb.

Far below in a deep valley was the evergreen forest, each tree clear, singular, and perfectly detailed, as though he might reach down and stir its needles. He imagined that if he jumped, he would land safely in a cushioned mattress of treetops.

From this height he enjoyed great vision. Ridge after ridge after countless ridge. The snow-white rock mountains were spotted here and there with solitary spruces and hemlocks. Great shadows, created by small frisky clouds, shifted like an artist's brush, daubing their snowy canvas purple and gray-green.

And beyond the mountains was an ocean! He could scarcely determine the ocean from the sky. Smooth blue clouds like whales flipped and swam through a purple sea sky. And the eagle soared above Harrison's head, showing off all the glory of The Highlands.

THE HIGHLANDS TUNNEL

24. ANSWERS

Brother came to stand beside him and survey the natural theatre of mountains and sea. He leaned his head back to the bright sky and saluted the eagle, who let out a wild, echoed greeting.

"It's stunning. . . ." Brother exclaimed, smiling up at the sky.

Harrison nodded, although he didn't think Brother was speaking to him but to the eagle. "Incredible," he breathed, sinking down to the rock ledge and hugging his knees to his chest.

He looked over to Brother who was suddenly seated, too.

"Sooo. . ." Harrison began, after a quiet moment, "what's this all about?"

Brother knew what his companion meant without requiring further explanation, and he didn't pretend not to know, which Harrison appreciated.

"We lost you," Brother said simply, with a slight smirk. "I thought it was time to call you back."

Harrison thought about the past couple of years. Disoriented, numb, dazed, preoccupied . . . he supposed

THE HIGHLANDS TUNNEL

he had been lost. It was like having amnesia of the present. With hindsight he realized that Brother's absence in the past was more deeply felt than Harrison's presence in his own life. He now sensed he was where he belonged. This is what it should have always been like. *I have come back from the dead!* Harrison silently exclaimed.

"But I don't want you to feel bad about being lost," Brother consoled. "Sometimes life gets really dark, we can't see anything, and we don't know where we're going. But, we are going, and at first, all we see is a pinpoint of light. So we move toward it and it grows until all at once, everything is illuminated."

Harrison was pleased to have received an answer—albeit a cryptic one. He decided to try for another.

"How did I get here? You know, when I exited the Mighty Midget Kitchen into the Crossing...."

"Well, there are lots of tunnels to The Highlands. Tunnels, bridges, doors . . . the portals are not even hidden—they're everywhere if you know how to look. They are disguised to most, because they are mysterious. Sometimes it's a person that gets you here. But you must be brave enough to go through the Crossing. That's the major block . . . besides that, people seem to ignore the tunnels."

"I wasn't looking for . . . a portal. I just stumbled in."

"Yes, well," Brother started sheepishly. "You were dissatisfied, which is a good place to start. But we had to lure you here. Sorry for that. Again."

"S'okay," Harrison assured. "Who are you? Not a Laoch, I know." For the same sort of obvious reason he knew Aubrey wasn't a Copy, he felt obligated to add, "You're not big enough." But Brother had seen combat, Harrison knew from the scars he had spied the night before.

"You're right. I'm not a Laoch. I'm not made like they are—not in the warrior sense, anyway. I don't fight . . . not yet, anyway. I'm the Ransom in all the old stories."

Then Brother rolled up his sleeve and unfastened the top couple buttons of his shirt at the collar so Harrison could see what had been hinted at in the firelight during the night before. Brother was cut, scarred—every bit of his skin was marked.

He huffed in surprise when he saw that a particularly jagged rip over Brother's heart had Harrison's name on it.

Too fascinated to look away, Harrison internally chided himself for staring. But no matter how he demanded, his eyes refused to obey his orders to look away. The scars were more beautiful than the mountain overlook they sat at. Brother, at least, didn't seem embarrassed.

"I'm sorry," Harrison muttered.

"Don't be. Scars are just reminders of where you used to hurt, but you don't anymore."

"Is this why I thought I knew you before? Because my name is on your body?"

"Yes. You knew me, but I can't introduce myself

properly unless you become open. We know each other well now, don't we?"

Harrison's brows knitted together soberly as he studied this new reveal. Maggie had called him "the hero" this morning. But Brother had named himself "the Ransom." Aubrey had told the story of the Ransom.

What might that mean? Harrison was quite familiar with the concept: a ransom was a price to be paid in exchange for something. How could a ransom be a hero? Brother was held ransom for some debt and he paid for it with his body?

"I paid for it with my life," Brother corrected, although Harrison had not spoken aloud.

He's dead, Harrison concluded. *I must be dead, too. Maggie was right.* Brother didn't automatically respond to these unspoken thoughts.

"You're a ghost?" Harrison asked finally. Then an idea came and he blurted it out before he could edit. "Are you my grandfather?"

"No, I'm not your grandfather. I'm not a ghost. Neither are you. See," and he took Harrison's hand and placed it on his chest. "You can breathe here."

Harrison exhaled in relief and nodded slowly. "What else do you want to know?" Brother offered.

"About the Copies," Harrison decided.

"Sure. Well, you know about Mrs. Byrne already. And her subordinate, the male, you know him."

"I do?"

"You helped create him."

"Oh?" That was unwelcome information.

"Everybody's got a Copy, Harrison. People are part light and part shadow," Brother said matter-of-factly. "We would like to blame something apart from us—the Unseen—but the truth is, we give the Enemy most of its ammunition. It's in us."

"I created a Copy . . . and his name is Curtis?"

Brother laughed. "Of course, that's not its real name. It's an alias, like Mrs. Byrne. Don't be offended, Harrison—your Copy is very evil, a worthy adversary. You created quite the monster."

"Thanks. . . ." Harrison replied, his voice trailing. He changed his mind and didn't want to think too much about his created Copy. That idea frightened him. Maybe another time, he elected.

"Tell me my name." He surprised himself with this request. It seemed his verbal filter had been turned off. Nonetheless, he had another name here, and he had heard it spoken. Brother had called him by his other name—his real name—during the bonfire.

"We use the Highland language here. Until you know the language, when I say your name, you won't understand its meaning."

"That's okay," he conceded. "I just need to hear it again."

Brother gave a nod and called him by name.

Harrison's eyes closed, and he half smiled. It sounded like a real warrior's name, like something from a storybook.

"What does it mean?" Harrison asked.

"That's hard to say. It doesn't translate well. The best I can come up with is . . . *Never.*"

Never. It spoke straight to Harrison's heart. *Yes*, he thought at first hearing. *That's it.*

But then he began to dismay. *Never* was a negative—it was hopeless, final.

"That's bad, isn't it?" He looked at Brother, imploring.

"Oh, it's very good. Like I said, it's the translation that's the problem. Sometimes the only accurate way something can be described is to use its negative. It's like—"

"It's like the Neverland," Harrison interrupted, his mind being abruptly invaded by the imaginary island from *Peter Pan.*

"Exactly. It's not supposed to be, but it is. You see, in all the great stories, there is truth. Technically speaking, 'never' means at no time in the past or future."

"Which puts us at now."

"Yes, now."

25. NOW

"So, now what do we do?" Harrison asked.

"Well, I reckon you've got more questions," Brother guessed.

"Yeah, but I don't want to miss out on any of this," he explained, waving at the world below.

"Ever been skreeing?" Brother asked, looking roguish, like he was enjoying some private joke.

"What?"

"Skree running? C'mon, I'll show you."

The two travelers stood up and with a slight incline of his head, Brother led Harrison back into the trees and down to another overlook. Before them stretched a hilly glacier that descended to the forest floor below.

"Follow me," Brother instructed over his shoulder. Then he took off running.

"Oh, I get it," Harrison mumbled to himself. "Not skiing—skreeing. Okay. Here goes."

He started the dash, slipping mostly on the icy surface of the slope. It wasn't a graceful descent, but it was really fun! Snowflakes burst from their feet and met in the cornflower blue sky, forming rows of wispy clouds.

The two skidded to a halt where the glacier leveled out. Neither skree-er was on his feet by the time they ran out of motion.

"I'm not very good at that," Harrison commented, laughing and lying on his back in the snow drift. Ice chips still swirled around his head from the action, some landing on his face where they quickly melted.

Brother joined his laughter. "No. Me neither."

Harrison considered Brother's appearance and manner as they lay side by side; the latter stayed still and obliging while his friend studied him. He was such a *man*. His hands looked appropriately capable and rough when gripping a rock ledge or even when holding that blasted knife. His able-bodied form—although not so broad, to the point of being labeled lanky—was such that made Harrison believe Brother could handle anything. He exuded masculinity, and to his new protégé, he really was the perfect big brother.

But last evening, Harrison noticed other attributes as well. Brother's long fingers and gentle touch ardently served food, caressed late-blooming flowers, and picked grass from Maggie's sweater. In fact, with Maggie, he sometimes seemed almost—well . . . motherly.

Brother turned his face toward Harrison and, as though he knew what he was thinking, allowed it to split into a wide grin, complete with mysterious glint in his eye. He looked almost proud. As minutes dragged by, it became apparent in the humored silence that he wasn't going to let Harrison in on the secret.

Then the atmosphere tangibly altered. The air seemed to gain weight swiftly and Brother's smile faded. It was the crash—the return to the valley, and Harrison intuited what was coming. His elation had reached unknown heights during his time here and the coming letdown would be devastating.

"Harrison, I need to talk to you," Brother said, sitting up on his elbows.

"Okay," he swallowed. "What about?"

"Your mission."

Maybe this won't be so bad, Harrison told himself. *I'm getting my orders*. But his initial suspicions were confirmed by Brother's next words.

"I'm sending you back."

He wasn't surprised by this revelation, but he reacted hotly, jerking himself up. "What? Why?"

"You need to get them back. They need you."

Harrison assumed that by "they," Brother meant Wheeler and Maggie.

"I need you there," Brother amended.

Harrison couldn't say anything; he knew this was his responsibility. But selfishly, he wanted to stay. For the first time since coming through the tunnel, he was starting to lose his temper.

"Could I come back?" he asked crossly.

"Of course, you'll come back," Brother reassured.

"So I escort Wheeler and Maggie back through the Crossing, then I can come back through the tunnel?"

"Think about it, Harrison. Could you say goodbye

to them so easily?"

A sharp ache stabbed his heart. No, he couldn't simply deposit them at the Mighty Midget and turn around. But now that he knew how to get here, perhaps he could come and go as he pleased.

"You don't have to go," Brother permitted, "but I want you to. I think you will want that, too . . . if later. There's something for you there, in the Practice World, and if you stay here, you miss out. This is important—*you're* important. So I'm asking you if you'll go. You accepted the mission last night. Part of that means going back."

"You don't want me," Harrison accused softly. Even as he said it, however, he knew it wasn't true.

Brother shook his head. "You don't know how hard it is for me to . . . physically be away from you. I like us to be like this. There's something better, though. But you need to go through with this first. You can't understand fully until we separate in this way. Please believe me."

Harrison took deep breaths through his nose. He was still angry.

"Fine. So what do I do?"

"Nothing. Just show up."

Well, that seemed anticlimactic. There must be more to it, Harrison suspected. Everything Brother said seemed to have a double meaning, but man, if Harrison didn't know what to make of this!

"Look, if you're angry, you can let me have it. Go ahead if it'll make you feel better. This is your choice, after all."

Harrison had wanted to refuse and throw out some profanity while he was at it, but now looking at the man—the man who had his name written over his heart—he really just wanted to say, "I love you, too." Because love was the unspoken message that radiated from Brother.

"So you'll go?" he asked with soft eyes.

"I don't know yet," Harrison replied honestly.

Brother nodded.

"I need to know what's there," Harrison continued. "I mean, what about the Unseen? Shouldn't we discuss strategy? The Enemy wants to kill me, and the Copies almost succeeded in doing just that. I don't want to return just to end up dead."

"I'll be with you . . . in a different way. I'm always with you, just not always like I am right now. But it's only your form that dies, Harrison. Besides, there's more at stake here than that."

"Oh, really? My identity, right? What I was made for?"

"That's right. That's something the Unseen wants you to forget. Forgetfulness is one of the Enemy's favorite weapons."

"So what was all of this for if I'm going back just to go back?" Harrison asked caustically.

"I already told you why you're here."

"So this was all just a reminder, a big do-over?"

"Is that so bad?"

He took a minute to think about it. "Guess not," he

finally conceded. "But what's it going to be like for me when I get back? Am I going to jail?"

"Look, you're telling yourself some story about what's going to happen when you return, but you don't know. Let's just focus on being here now. We have more time before the train leaves. I'd like to make the most of it."

When Brother stood up, Harrison moved to stand. Brother offered a hand.

"The thing is, the Practice World that you live in isn't reality. It's an imperfect reflection. The Unseen has distorted it. He made its inhabitants forget their real home. So, forgetting what they were made for, the people make choices that set things more and more out of sync with reality. You are real, but what you can't see is more reality than what you can.

"So, with the Practice World, you must take the good and the bad—accept all of it. Because, that's the way it's set up. And life in the Practice World is essential. You can experience it just as you do here."

They started to walk, the mood lifting slightly.

"But like the train, life doesn't just stop when it's not supposed to . . . and it doesn't take detours. You're supposed to be there for now."

There was that word again. *Now.*

"Well, since I'm here *now*, I have more questions," Harrison said.

"Shoot."

"Maggie. She stole this knife. And she lied about it. I don't know what to do with that. I mean, I helped her get away with it."

"She did not steal the knife," Brother said flatly.

"But it was in her pocket," Harrison protested. "Nobody planted it on her either—she had a hand in her pocket almost the whole time. I would have seen it."

"That man made the whole thing up."

Harrison thought back to the scene in the tent and pictured the boisterous vendor in his head. "He made up the . . . what, the theft?"

"He gave her the knife before you saw her. It was all plotted. He wasn't working alone."

"What, it's like a conspiracy theory? Is he a Copy?"

"No, but believe me, the Copies are in on it. What did Maggie tell you?"

Harrison thought back to the conversation in the caboose. "She said he gave it to her."

"That's true, and it's not finished. I think you should talk to Maggie about it."

"All right, I will," Harrison promised. Perhaps this was the important mission. Maggie's safety was definitely worth the trip back through the Crossing.

THE HIGHLANDS TUNNEL

26. PERSPECTIVE

"Come on. I promise I will explain everything soon. Follow me."

"Where are we going?"

"We need a change of perspective. I want to show you the beach."

Harrison accompanied Brother into the forest, and as they stepped through the snow-carpeted woods, his mood changed. He felt different . . . respectful in a way. The red-barked trees seemed to reach as high as the mountain they had climbed. Sunlight fell in slanted green-yellow beams through tree branches, pooling on the ground like heavenly spotlights.

He felt lighter and taller—wonderstruck when he comprehended his connection to this ancient, magical world. He was a part of this everlasting realm; he belonged here. That was certain. No doubt he would carry this place with him even in the peaks and valleys of the Practice World.

Harrison looked up into the boughs of the evergreens, which were being stirred by a spry breeze. He was eternal, but he was also becoming new. Like this land.

Then he smelled the ocean.

Soon the two journeyers emerged from the forest onto a rocky shoreline, where wild waves chased sea birds and churned up on the sand. Tree-topped islands emerged like stepping stones out in the water. It was frosty, but the snow had melted under the sun on the beach.

Brother and Harrison wandered along without talking, picking up stones that caught their eye and pieces of driftwood. The magic was deep here, too. Harrison felt worshipful—like the waves—drawn out from himself into the presence of something bigger.

"When you come back, I'm going to take you sailing and hang-gliding here," Brother was saying.

Hang-gliding. *Flying*. Harrison was high on the promise.

"There's more here that I look forward to showing you, too," Brother hinted. "Beyond the ocean and over the mountain ranges. Other lands and cities. . . ."

"Cities?" That was hard to imagine. Cities must be built. And surely a city would be inhabited by people. The parts of The Highlands Harrison had visited were so natural and isolated.

"Yeah," Brother answered. "And there are other beings besides humans and Laochs."

"Like what?"

"Ah, well, there is the smaller version of the Laochs. No bigger than children. Very charming. People always love them."

"When will I get to meet them?"

"Soon." He leaned in to Harrison. "I only show you what you give me permission to show you. You see what you want to see here. It's very personal; I make it that way for you. This land is where you recover things you might have lost, or see actualized the dreams that got away from you."

He was looking impish again. "But I can blow your mind, if you let me."

The horse was unexpectedly walking beside him on the rocky beach, and it nudged Harrison with its nose.

"Do you want to ride?" Brother asked him.

He answered that he did feel inclined to ride, although he wasn't tired of walking. His legs and feet felt as strong as they had that morning. But the horse's body was warm and sturdy under him. The rocking of forward motion combined with the steady air expanding its belly lured Harrison into an easy sleep, during which he dreamed of spring.

When he awoke they were in the clearing again, and Maggie and Wheeler were there with Aubrey and Calista and the other Laochs. The train had come back. He hoped Maggie and Wheeler weren't cross for being left all day.

"Hey, Harrison!" Wheeler called. He didn't sound put out fortunately.

Harrison slid off the back of the horse and nodded his thanks to the animal, then met the others. He only noticed that his boots were missing when his feet hit the snow.

"Today was so cool," Wheeler said excitedly.

"Oh? Well, good. What did you do?" Harrison queried, feeling better about having been gone.

"I spent the day with Brother. We did amazing things."

Harrison raised an eyebrow at the aforementioned, who shrugged and feigned innocence.

"Yeah, so did I," he admitted slowly, not sure what to make of that. "What did you do?"

"Mostly we wrestled." Of course that would be what Wheeler would want to do. He was always trying to wrestle his big brother at home. "And we built some forts in the woods out of logs."

"And we talked," Maggie said, approaching with bright eyes.

"*You* talked," Brother clarified. "I listened." She swatted at his arm, but he dodged and smirked at her.

There was more that wasn't being said—Harrison could tell when he examined Maggie's and Wheeler's faces—more to their journeys that day than the stated activities. But it was private—between Brother and the individual. Harrison knew he felt that way, too, so he didn't pry.

Maggie stretched up on her toes next to Brother and he bent lower so she could speak in his ear. Her eyes were all of a sudden filled with tears.

"You, love, were worth it," Brother replied to her inaudible whisper.

"What's up, Harrison?" Wheeler asked, noticing his

brother's bewildered expression.

Harrison looked at Brother while he answered Wheeler's question. "Just wondering how Brother spent the entire day with all three of us separately."

"It's magic, Harrison," Maggie said, rolling her eyes. "Can you handle that?"

"I'm handling this all just fine," he assured. "But would Brother, Aubrey, or somebody kindly tell us when the train is leaving. I've got to get you two back home safely."

Maggie glared contemptuously at Harrison, and Wheeler's mouth dropped open.

"What? No! I don't want to go back."

"Come on, Wheeler. You know we can't stay here. We've got parents, who will worry—"

"And a heck of a lot of trouble!" Wheeler exclaimed.

"Don't worry," Maggie muttered. "It's not your trouble."

Aubrey made a noise like to clear his throat—but it was obviously unnecessary and an attempt to take the floor, so it came out sounding exactly like "Ahem." They all looked up at him expectantly. "Your train will be leaving tonight," he announced regretfully.

Harrison was resigned. Maggie and Wheeler looked defeated until Brother spoke up.

"You will see spring here in The Highlands. I promise. I can't wait to show you the thunderstorms."

Their hearts lightened some with that promise. It was sunset again in the meadow, and the beauty was heartbreaking. The coral sky was reflected in the snow, which shimmered in the dusky light.

"There is still much time before your departure," Aubrey told them, "and we will first sit down to a meal."

As it happened, the humans were rather hungry and eagerly welcomed dinner.

"Supper tonight was catered by a friend from the Practice World," Brother explained. "Which brings me to your surprise. . . ." He smiled enigmatically and pointed to the west.

Harrison squinted and was barely able make out a tall, slender silhouette against the blazing sunset. As the figure came closer, he saw that the man wore a soldier's garrison cap and belted uniform jacket. Just then, a low bark announced the body of a large dog headed over the hill for the meadow.

Harrison recognized the Great Dane before he did the man, but its identity helped clear it all up for him.

"Who is that?" Wheeler asked.

"It's our grandfather," Harrison revealed with narrow eyes. He was not certain how he knew, but in that instant it all came together.

Sure enough, the man approached the Bentley brothers and smiled. He was young and clad in an officer's uniform—pilot's wings on the lapel. He took his hat off to display a head of thick dark hair.

Wheeler gasped when he recognized this fellow as not only his grandfather but as Harold from the Mighty Midget Kitchen.

27. WAR STORY

Harrison stared at Brother with an open mouth—confusion and not a little outrage wreaking havoc inside of him.

"I thought it was time you boys hear the whole story," Brother inclined his head toward Harold, "from the man who was there to experience it."

"The man who watches you in secret," the officer clarified, brows brought together apologetically. "For that distance, I hope you'll forgive me."

His expression was a disturbing mixture of sorrow, contrition, and longing, but Harrison wasn't going to give him the reward of his forgiveness yet. Distance was fine with him; he wished the man would continue to keep his distance.

Then Harold's forehead eased and his tone lightened. "But before we get to all the gory details, how about we eat!" He clapped Brother's shoulder and the two shared a look filled with an intimacy and familiarity that Harrison envied.

The Laochs had set up a marquee in the meadow that

was crowded inside with tables and benches. Harold had provided excellent barbeque and yeast rolls with sides of mac and cheese and what looked to be fried green beans (these Harrison found surprisingly tasty). The soldier may have prepared the meal, but Brother insisted on serving.

Woodland animals joined the gathering again this evening, although their dinners varied. The band was jamming to a catchy rhythm, and the Laochs looked to be enjoying their costume party for a second time. They had traveled to the Practice World and back this day but appeared well kempt and urbane as always, despite the battle.

Harrison—although twisted up by the tangible presence of this fresh young soldier, the man who embodied a shameful legend in their family—kept an eye on Maggie, who was sitting on one of the tables talking to Brother.

The latter, having finished his meal—which he had eaten enthusiastically—sat on the table behind Maggie's back, casually weaving her black hair into a long braid. His face was alight with whatever she was sharing with him. Like a gentleman, he never interrupted and only voiced a question or an encouragement to continue. Calista sat on the bench in front of the pair, listening and sharing, totally focused on Maggie. The girl seemed to be soaking up all the attention. Harrison supposed she was being diverted so he and Wheeler could get their time in with Harold.

The two brothers sat across from their grandfather

and ate, impressed by his sharp uniform and youthful good looks. He was sharing his plate with the Great Dane, who sat at the table beside him. The horse stood by, as was customary, its large head bobbing amicably between Harrison and Wheeler. Wheeler offered it pieces of his roll, which it nibbled greedily.

"So . . . you've been dead for a long while now. How's that going?" Wheeler asked, uninhibited as usual. "You are dead, right?"

Young Harold chuckled. "Yes, it's several decades since I died in the Practice World. You see, though," he enthused, holding up his hands, "I'm more alive now than ever."

"That sounds like a contradiction," Harrison accused—respectfully, of course.

Harrison's emotions flitted from tenderness to offense, from rapture to indignation. Presented before him was the physical manifestation of a man he had despised and scorned since he was old enough to understand what treachery was. And yet here was the man for whom he was named. The missing man. . . .

"I'm more authentic now, I suppose I should say," Harold amended.

"Well, that's even harder to believe," his skeptical grandson countered. "It seems to me you spend most of your time hiding. You pretend to be the hot dog man," he reminded.

"Yes. Well, that's so I can interact in the Practice World. I go where my family goes. Remember I told you my diner was at Union Station?"

THE HIGHLANDS TUNNEL

"You know, I've been fixing your dad's hot dogs since before you were born," Harrison recalled Harold saying.

The man's face fell suddenly. "I know what you were told about me," he said. "I don't know what you think about it—I can imagine, to be sure—but I do think you'll want to hear my story."

Wheeler nodded enthusiastically. Harrison wasn't so keen, but he did want to hear the truth. He dipped his head sternly once for Harold to proceed. The young man shifted in his seat, sitting straighter and more formally, representing a trained officer of the United States military.

And with that, their grandfather began his tale.

"When the war started, I joined the American Air Corps. I had my pilot's license already and had been flying for several years, so I was assigned to pilot a B-17 bomber. Mostly milk runs to France, but a few rather terrifying missions with heavy flak and enemy fighters. I flew twenty-some successful bombings during my first tour. I was even awarded a couple of medals. I can tell you about those excursions another time; I think the following account will mean the most to you.

"It was called to the attention of my higher-ups that I spoke several languages fluently. This was thanks to my mother," Harold said in an aside, "who made sure my upbringing included foreign language, fencing, horsemanship, and music. Even though flying and cooking were my chief passions." He chuckled.

"The officials told her that I had been selected for another tour of duty, piloting the bomber again. However, I had no real crew, no real plane. It was a cover story and something to put down on paper. The military instead gave me a new identity and sent me into enemy territory."

"You mean you were a spy?" Wheeler cut in.

"I was. I was trained to speak the enemy's language—essentially to *be* the enemy. I had fake foreign documents assigned to me . . . even a new phony pilot license and a false degree from their university. I was accepted into their ranks. I had a menial with the military, but eventually their leaders learned to trust me.

"I think I was good at following orders, blending in, pretending to be something I wasn't." Here, he looked at Harrison. "I did what was expected of me. But you see, I also spoke French, which was discovered by my new overseer. So, the enemy made me their spy, too. Before I knew it, I was operating as a double agent. Of course, France was allied with the Americans and the British, so I was telling my secrets to the French as well. It made my job more efficient, and my real employers were quite pleased with my promotion.

"It was in France that I met your grandmother. Her older brother was a leader of the Resistance. We fell in love, and. . . . Well, this is another story for another time . . . maybe when you're older." He winked. Wheeler pretended to faint.

"Anyway, I felt like a marionette being pulled by two puppeteers. I think I got fed up of being told what to do all the time. And although I did not have the permission of my government, I married her first chance we got. We spent several weekends together, when I wasn't reporting back to either the Allies or the enemy.

"When my higher-ups on the American front found out what I had done, they obviously didn't approve. They knew I couldn't afford any significant relationships. And being related to a Resistance leader made it especially dangerous. If the enemy found out about her and discovered my guise, they would find her and use her to get information from me. Of course, I said I would never let it get that far; I had plans to end my life if I was apprehended in that way—we all carried cyanide in the event of capture. But the thought of the enemy getting to her. . . . Well, I couldn't allow that.

"Foolishly, I kept a photograph of Josephine in my hat. But it was all I had of her to take with me, and I didn't think any harm would come of it. How would anybody know who she was, anyway? It wasn't labeled, and I left all of our letters, written in French, back at our room in Paris.

"One evening, I was in a meeting with my enemy leaders, relaying information from my time with the Resistance. Known to be a pilot, I was ordered to fly a small plane back to France with another officer, who also spoke French and served as an intelligence expert. I was happy to go back because I had learned from my American contacts that Jo was with child.

"During our flight, this man—the intelligence officer—was in the back of the plane where I had stowed my coat and hat, and he found the photograph. When I turned around in the cockpit, I was horrified to notice him back there going through my things. He held the picture in his hand, and I saw it clear as day in his expression when he recognized her, because he glanced up at me with blame in his eyes. I later learned that he shared the same print in *his* files, due to her brother's role in the Resistance. The whole family was documented.

"Then I had to make a choice, and it was a simple one at that. Simple, but not easy. I deliberated for maybe twenty minutes, quickly tallying up my options.

"I could kill the man and make it look like an accident, then return to the enemy. I failed, however, to come up with a proper explanation that would protect myself from suspicion. I would no doubt face scrutiny, which I did not need, and this would ultimately get me in trouble.

"I thought again that I could kill the man, then fly to fetch Jo, and disappear. Still, I knew too much for the enemy to just let me go. We would be pursued, and until when? I had no idea how long the wretched war would last.

"I wanted very badly to make the scheduled landing in France, finish our mission, say my goodbye to Josephine—to see her one last time. Then I would crash our plane on the return flight. All the same, the officer knew my secret and . . . he knew that I knew that he knew. I couldn't risk his contacting our headquarters in the meantime, or trying something on me and leaving my new wife unprotected."

Harold, watching his story play out on a private screen, had broken eye contact with his grandsons.

"There was one option left the way I saw it. I had to destroy us. For the sake of Josephine and our unborn baby. So I kept the plane headed toward our destination, but when I located a barren field, I drove it straight to the ground. I couldn't allow any room for error. We both had to die, and the contents of the plane had to burn.

"My body must have broken on impact . . . but it was in the crash, in the burning that—" Harold stammered to a stop, trying to find words the boys would understand. Until this point in the story, he was able to relate the events without being affected by them, which Harrison thought curious. But at this stage, the soldier was almost overtaken by emotion.

"As we plunged, I saw," he gulped. "I saw . . . the Giver. An immense light . . . and clarity . . . and beauty . . . and arms. The Giver held arms open in welcome. I was aware of the explosion, but I felt no pain, only satisfaction and relief. When I saw the Giver, I knew I belonged in this service. There was no going back."

He leaned forward, close to the boys, as if divulging a special secret. "Once you see the Giver, you don't want anything else in all the universe."

28. THE TRUTH

"If I had only known that underneath the façade of this conflict was an even larger theatre of war, a battle that had been raging since the beginning of time. . . ." He shook his head, as if to say, *How could I not have known?* "So, The Highlands needed a spy—somebody to work in the Practice World on the human side. Somebody to protect the openings to The Highlands, because the Unseen would love nothing more than to see those doors locked and forgotten. And that's my assignment. I help to keep the openings accessible."

Brother cut in, having without notice joined their table. "That's an important job, you see, because people don't want to leave their so-called 'safe' boundaries. Harry provides a way in and the encouragement to take the risk."

An important job. It resonated with Harrison, who was asked to go back to the Practice World for an important reason. Perhaps he would take after his grandfather after all.

He wasn't sure exactly at what point in the story his perception of Harold had improved. His prejudices started to break down when he heard that his grandfather had been a spy. And his great-uncle—who did not survive the war either—was a leader of the Resistance! He must be in The Highlands, too. This was a lot of legacy to absorb in one moment.

The Rider had stayed close to Harrison throughout the story time, although his body sat some distance away with Maggie. This was the first time Harrison had been aware of Brother's attention when he wasn't physically nearby.

"But your granddad here does a bang-up job of it," Brother was saying. "The Copies are terrified of him."

"Well, I was taught by the best," Harry complimented humbly, although his expression was proud.

Then he gazed at the Bentley brothers with fondness.

"I've watched you close. I *know* you. I've been your grandfather all along, but you didn't know me. Even though I was right with you the whole time, you were so separate from my reality that you didn't know I was there. And I've missed you for that. It didn't work out the way one would think it's supposed to, but I was promised this reunion. No, I suppose 'reunion' is the wrong word. I was promised this *introduction*. I have looked forward to this day for many decades. When I could see you here, and you could see me for who I am. The anticipation's kept me content to be 'the hot dog man' all these years."

"But didn't you want the truth to be told? I mean, everybody thinks you're a traitor," Harrison reasoned, thinking that would be his chief concern.

"Yes, but mostly I missed the opportunity to be present with you. I've spent much time with your grandmother, when she is sleeping or knitting quietly or taking a walk . . . I've even shown myself to her a couple of times. But it's not the same. And dear girl, she never believed the story they told her."

"But didn't she know you were a spy? She must have known," Wheeler insisted.

Young Harold shook his head. "No. I made sure she didn't know anything. I would have never let her be endangered by the knowledge of my connections. She knew about her brother's cause, but that was all. She thought I flew bombers, just like the rest of my family. She thought I was stationed in England and came to Paris on my leave."

"But why did they say what they did? They could have made up something a little less awful," Harrison claimed.

"I suppose it was an easy explanation. It was something that happened, you know. Men jumping ship for Switzerland. And, they didn't have a body . . . the plane and the crew didn't exist. But the military did get your grandmother safely to the States, and I'm grateful for that. I don't care what story they had to make up."

"When she sees you—like you said you show yourself to her . . . um, does she know it's you?" Harrison wanted to know.

"Yes, I'm certain she knows."

"But then if she sees you, wouldn't she think that

you did bail out and abandoned her?"

"Jo sees me as a young man. Like the last day she saw me alive. I don't age for her. I don't know what she thinks when she sees me. That I'm a ghost, probably . . . that I'm a creation of her imagination or product of loneliness . . . I don't know. But she knows I didn't abandon her. I can feel that much. All I can say is, whenever I'm near her, a connection is made, or some supernatural level is crossed. Our love manifests in a way that makes it almost touchable."

Harrison was deeply affected by the essence of Harold's action. "You sacrificed your life for us. Because she lived, we're alive . . . and it's all because you died."

"I would do it again every day of eternity," Harry exclaimed with a grin.

"You said that you later found out that the man recognized our grandmother's picture. How later?" Wheeler asked.

"Well, I talked to the man about it. His name is Stefan. He's a good friend."

The brothers looked at each other and then back at their grandfather.

"But you killed him!" Wheeler objected.

"Yes, well, he understands. Just as I understand his choices. He's very content with his lifestyle in The Highlands. After meeting the Giver, he didn't want it any other way."

"The enemy is in The Highlands. . . ." Wheeler trailed off, misunderstanding.

"Oh, Stefan is not the enemy," Brother explained,

as if talking about an old buddy. "Never was. Now, the real Enemy is not here; but only because of a general distaste for the place."

"So, in the Practice World," Harrison tried to clarify with his grandfather, "you're Harold running a little take-out diner. And here you're—"

"Harry, like I told you before. I happen to look like this here, but in the Practice World, I use my disguise, which is the same as this, only aged appropriately. Different costume, too."

"You're a spy for the Giver?"

"Yes, sort of. It makes me happy . . . what I do. It's what I was made for."

"And you said before that you made hot dogs for my dad since before I was born. Did you used to cook for him when the Mighty Midget was in Washington?"

"Yup. He used to come to the train station for my hot dogs."

"Did he ever know?"

"No, he thought it was a coincidence, my moving to Grant," Harry said with a grimace. Then he leaned in closer, white teeth gleaming. "But I'm mighty proud of him, as I am of you two. I'm a regular granddad." This sounded inconsistent coming from a man who looked to be no older than twenty-five. "Just ask Brother. I brag on you fellows all the time." He winked.

"And I'm just as bad as he is," Brother admitted.

"We're just so happy to have you here," Harry whispered.

"I—I just," Harrison stuttered, looking at Brother

for help. "I just can't believe it. I mean, I've hated you my whole life," he blurted out defenselessly.

"Well, now, I can't blame you for that. I don't want you to feel bad. Now you know the truth."

"Do you know what my dad thinks about you? He's never really said."

"I don't know what he believes. But he named you after me; he mustn't think too badly of me."

Unless he thinks badly of me, Harrison thought.

Brother frowned and looked at him, disappointed. "I wanted you both to be here for this, because it will change things for you. It's not always like this, though. There are things that are really awful—wicked, unlucky, less-than-heroic things that happen in life. In those situations, there is also truth that changes perception, but it's not always as obvious as it is in Harry's story. Do you understand that?"

The boys nodded.

So my dad hates me. Great! What truth can change that? Harrison mused again.

But then he allowed for a more pleasing idea. His grandmother believed better of her husband; perhaps she had passed that esteem on to her son.

"I need to know something else," Wheeler interjected. "What's it like to be dead?"

His grandfather considered that. "I suppose it's the same as being alive—but with endless possibilities and greater vision."

"Is there anything I can tell *Grand-mere* for you?" Harrison asked thoughtfully, wondering just how he would convey correspondence from a dead man.

Harold accepted gratefully. "Tell her to be at peace, because I am. And tell her thanks for believing." He swallowed his emotion and continued in a trembling voice. "Tell her that I never left her and I love her."

"I will," Harrison promised, nodding. Then he remembered. "What about my father?"

"Oh, yes! Tell him . . . that I'm sorry he's not known me. Tell him that I'm proud of him. That I love him. And that he's raised two fine lads." Harold's eyes twinkled with truth.

Harrison's smiled, but it faded fast. "I'm being sent back home, so I can pass on your messages. Before I get shipped off to military school or the juvenile detention facility, that is."

His grandfather picked up on the disappointment under the sarcasm. "You will be back. You were meant to fly, Harrison. It's in your blood."

Harrison's mouth and eyes opened in surprise. Inside he was soaring.

THE HIGHLANDS TUNNEL

29. ENJOY

Aubrey approached the company and gave a short bow.

"Sirs. It is time to head out for the train stop."

"Of course," Brother agreed. "Let's go collect your shoes." He nodded to Harold, Wheeler, and Harrison.

They assembled a hiking party that included Maggie, Aubrey, Juda, Calista, and the horse.

Harrison felt the change happening inside of him. It was the benefit of knowing his namesake's identity—with that knowledge he was beginning to understand who he was. His grandfather was a hero, and he shared his name . . . and personality. He could hope he shared a similar destiny.

Once in the dark of the forest, the rest moved ahead faster, while Brother held Harrison back a distance.

"Thanks for that," he told Brother, meaning the time with his grandfather.

"My pleasure. We all have to contend with false stories. Sometimes it's the true stories and family histories that haunt us. But the truth is so much better. And by the way, your father didn't name you after his father to torture you. Much the opposite actually."

Oh. . . . That was good. If Brother said so, Harrison believed it. He would be telling his dad about Harold when he got back home. "Brother? Is any of this a secret? You know, like I shouldn't talk about it. . . ."

"Oh, no. It's not a secret. Share at your discretion. It's your story to tell."

"All right. I will."

"Harrison, there's more you need to know about going back."

"Okay." When Brother didn't speak, he questioned. "What is it?"

"Maggie will be leaving the Practice World soon to join us here in The Highlands," Brother stated solemnly, keeping his blue eyes locked on Harrison's face.

"What's that supposed to mean?" he shot back, eyes jerking up to meet Brother's. The exhilaration that came with hearing Harold's story was snuffed out like a falling star.

"It just means that you should enjoy her now."

What? Was that supposed to make it okay?

"Can't you stop it?" he shouted, not caring if the others could hear.

"People make choices. I can't stop that. I'm bound in those ways. I can change the inside . . . with permission. Only you can change your path."

Harrison looked up through the pine branches to the sky, eyes darting from one corner of the expanse to the other, looking for an argument, a loophole. He remembered the way Brother looked at her, the girl tucked into his side.

He wants her to himself, he thought. *And he wants me gone.* Harrison gripped the knife in his pocket violently. Distrust filtered through his core. *Why should I trust this guy anyway? I don't even really know who he is or what this is about. He may have brainwashed me, for all I know. Or slipped me a magic mushroom . . . or something!*

But when he gazed again at the Rider, he remembered. His name was written over the man's heart. Somewhere along the way, Brother had taken a hit for him. He obviously didn't deserve Harrison's anger. The boy's shock and fury turned quite suddenly to grief.

"Not Maggie," he groaned. "No! I can't accept this."

"It's just her form, Harrison. That's not such a terrible thing, is it?"

"Stop saying that! She's just a girl! Can't you let her be?" He gulped the highland air as he argued in his head. *Let her grow up, for God's sake. Graduate school, fall in love, have babies—grandbabies even!* Harrison, surprising himself, imagined being by her side at each of these events.

"Take me instead," Harrison begged.

"I have greater things in mind, Harrison," Brother whispered, a storm developing in the harbor of his eyes. "Believe me."

Greater things. Something important, right? That's what Brother had said. Like Harold's important job.

"I want to believe," Harrison whispered, thinking he sounded ridiculously like the main character from a popular television show he used to watch with his dad.

"It's not a job so much," Brother said, revising the boy's unspoken thoughts. "It's more like a place for you . . . a part to play."

Harrison explored Brother's expression. The man was hurting. He was also desperately willing Harrison to understand something.

And then Harrison got it.

Or he thought he did.

He was supposed to protect Maggie. He could change his path, Brother had said. Perhaps he could change things for Maggie. This was life or death. Like Harold had sacrificed his life for his young wife and child. This was Harrison's mission. He carried the knife in his pocket. He hadn't fought for her yesterday, but by God, he would fight for her today.

"Am I going to do this right?" Harrison asked for what seemed like the thousandth time.

"Not always," Brother replied, purposefully answering another sense of the question. "You're going to leave me sometimes. You will chase other . . . distractions. See, I'm in a rather sorry position. I want you forever, but you might not always want me."

"No, no, no, no. . . ." the boy moaned.

"It's all well. I'll keep waiting, and I will chase after you when I can. I'm completely besotted with you, Harrison. I really have no choice but to pursue you. And you will get a lot of things right."

"How?"

"Stay with me," Brother responded simply with a crooked smile.

"I can't," he answered, bemused. "I've got to go on the train. You're not coming. . . . You told me to go."

"I know, but if you want me with you, I will be with you."

Harrison thought about that and wondered how it would work.

"I want you with me," he admitted.

"I want to be with you," Brother answered.

Feeling a clutter of emotion, Harrison promptly reached out to Brother, who grabbed him in a fierce embrace.

The sensation clasped onto words and they spilled from the boy's mouth, a duet with the tears from his eyes. "I'm sorry I didn't trust you. I will now. I'm not angry. I just want to do this right. I can climb, and I can fight. But this, this important thing. . . . Am I going to get that right?" he asked again with desperation.

"I love you," Brother whispered in response, not letting go.

"I love you, too." And he did. Was that honestly the answer to all his questions and doubts?

"All right?" Brother asked, when Harrison pulled away. Harrison saw the tears in Brother's eyes, which seemed to validate his own. *The ghost cries*, he thought.

"I'm ready. Let's get them on the train."

"Harrison?"

"Yeah?"

"You are worth the chase any day," Brother told him, looking impossibly wolfish.

THE HIGHLANDS TUNNEL

30. DEPARTURE

The train was waiting when they arrived, puffing and gleaming in the last light of day. The passengers took the last steps from out of the trees and gaped at its polished beauty.

Maggie started to trip on the deeply grooved terrain that ran next to the tracks. The horse steadied her with nudges, offering a sturdy neck to grasp, and Harrison again was curious about the pocked ground.

"Where did they go?" Wheeler asked.

The other two looked around and saw that, besides their equine companion, they were alone.

"I thought that Calista would go with us," Maggie said, confused and rather hurt.

Harrison, too, had assumed the Laochs, or at least Harold, would take the train back to the Crossing with them.

It was a great disappointment, and yet, all three felt a twinge of relief that they wouldn't have to say goodbye. A farewell at this point would have been traumatic.

"Mythical beings. So unpredictable," Wheeler

mock-accused.

Harrison figured he knew why they had been left alone to board. "It's our choice to go back. They don't want to make us, and I guess their being here would make it feel sort of pressured."

"Yeah, they didn't want to railroad us," Wheeler snorted, trying out a pun, which was ignored by the other two in the melancholy evening light.

"So, are we all agreed? Are we going back?" the oldest brother posed.

The matter was settled for Harrison; he was getting on the train. As far as he was concerned, Maggie and Wheeler would be getting on board, too, but he thought it polite to make it seem like they had their choice as well.

He watched them carefully. Wheeler looked back into the woods and at the horse. Maggie studied the ground, biting her lip.

"Maggie," he said, beginning with—he concluded—the more resistant personality. "Think of your father. He can't lose you."

"But Brother. . . ." she murmured, forlorn. All at once, her dark eyes met his defiantly.

"He's not here," Harrison said quickly. "What Wheeler said is the truth. You can't control him."

"I can," she said petulantly. "He'll come back if I ask him to."

Oh, gosh, she might be right. Harrison hadn't thought about her calling him back. That would be bad; if she summoned Brother, he would definitely come back, and then it would be impossible to leave with Maggie.

"Maybe. But don't do that." Harrison struggled for a reason. "It will be awkward."

He gently continued to remind her of what was at stake. "Your father. Everything your father's done has been for you. He carried you on his back across a desert and a river to get you to safety, so that he could stay with you. Be with him, Maggie. Brother is with us. He's not going to leave you, but he wants you to do what's important and right."

Harrison's voice was full of a tenderness that was somewhat out of character for him.

He saw her soften and resolve to depart. Maggie nodded her assent.

Wheeler was stubborn, too.

"Harrison, we don't have to leave. Why would we?"

The engine let out a loud, fussing hiss of steam. It was ready to depart.

"If I'm going, you're going, too. I'm not returning to Mom and Dad without you. How could you do that to them?"

"Then stay with me," he pleaded.

"And let them lose two sons? Wheeler, that's beyond cruel. What about *Grand-mere?* She already lost our grandfather. You wouldn't want to make her suffer like that again."

Harrison was ready to tackle him if Wheeler tried to make off. He didn't want to do it that way, but he would to save his family the grief that his grandmother had suffered forty-some years before when her husband and the father of her unborn baby never returned home from war.

Wheeler hung his head when he realized that arguing was futile. It was impossible to stay because they were expected at home . . . they had been expected yesterday for dinner. His head snapped up when the coupling rods on the train's wheels began their pushing and pulling, causing the machine to roll.

The horse was neighing and bucking its head.

"We can come back here, though," Wheeler remembered suddenly. "Brother said we would see spring in The Highlands. And he said we could come to the victory party when the war ends."

"That's right," Harrison quickly confirmed, grabbing at Maggie. He eagerly pushed her and Wheeler toward the steps of the next passing car.

Once on the steps, they all three looked back at the horse, which had started to trot alongside. It picked up its pace as the train did until it was running at a full gallop beside them. It whinnied and shook its head as it ran, black mane flouncing in the air like billowing steam.

Wheeler leaned out and stroked its hair while Harrison held on to his jacket. Maggie was in tears again, muttering to the horse in Spanish, and Harrison held up his hand in a pathetic wave. The kids hated to leave as much as it seemed the horse hated to let them go. Eventually, however, the creature stopped and stood watching its three friends retreat into the distance, its breath escaping its nostrils in ephemeral clouds.

"Goodbye," Harrison whispered. "Thank you."

When the horse was out of sight, they collected themselves and turned to the interior of the car. It was a passenger coach with a glass roof that allowed an unobscured view of The Highlands sky. Maggie was the first into the lounge.

"There you are!" she shouted. The brothers jumped up swiftly from the outside steps and subsequent landing, alarmed by her odd outburst.

They entered just in time to see Maggie slapping the chest of the nearest Laoch, who happened to be Juda. They all laughed—they being the aforementioned tall guy along with Aubrey, Calista, and young Harold.

Even though Harrison was used to the Laochs by now, they were as-ever intimidating, and he was horrified to see Maggie hit one. Still, he sighed with the comfort of seeing them again.

"We thought you left without saying goodbye." She waved an accusing finger at them with a ferocity that was both feminine and Latin.

"We apologize, madame," Aubrey stated in his lovely up-and-down accent, which made the word *apologize* sound like its own song. "We had to leave you for a moment, as Brother needed us. But we are here now."

Harrison noticed Maggie's glower soften at the mention of Brother's name. She was still sulking about being made to leave, nonetheless.

"You're coming with us? To the Practice World?" Harrison asked.

"We'll come part of the way," Harry explained, "but we're not scheduled to go all the way to the Practice World until tomorrow."

"That's okay. We're happy to see you," Harrison said.

"And we are happy to see you on this train," Aubrey replied. "We thought maybe you would change your mind and decide to stay. But Brother said you would follow through with the plan."

"You ought not to second-guess Brother," Harry told him with half a smile.

"After all our time together, you would think we would learn that."

"Come on! Even I know that," Wheeler said, his mood having improved with the surprise company.

"Well, that's very wise," Juda commended.

"Aww, you big lug. I knew you wouldn't leave me. All right. So is there anything to eat in the dining car?" Wheeler questioned, getting down to his foremost inclination.

"Just might be, partner," Juda said. "I'll take you."

"I'll go, too," Harry offered, "in case my services are needed."

The remaining passengers settled in—Maggie retreated to the back with Calista, and Aubrey sat looking meaningfully at Harrison. There was still more to be discussed. Harrison nodded and made his way to Aubrey's side.

31. Last Discussions

"You look ready, Harrison," Aubrey said approvingly.

"Really?" *Ready for what?* "What am I ready for, Aubrey? What am I going to do when I get back?"

"This is not about anything you must do. Remember that. What I meant by ready was . . . complete. You are you again."

"I feel changed."

"You are not a different man, but you are new again."

"Aubrey? I still don't know who the Giver is."

"Yes, you do," he countered simply. "You met the Giver."

"Who is it?"

"The Giver is all of this," Aubrey said, using his hands to illustrate. "The Highlands. This train. The meadow. The mountain. The fire. The Giver is in it all. Brother is the Giver, and the Giver lives inside of you."

And then he understood. The horse, the bear, the eagle . . . even the snarling coyote. The horse came with a rider. When the animals came in pairs, one was the Giver and the other was Brother.

"The ground along the tracks is marked by the Giver's hooves," Harrison said.

"The horse runs alongside the railroad when the Giver is anticipating the return of one of The Highlands citizens. Where the train stops is the very ground where Brother returned from the Practice World after his sacrifice long ago. It is a place of great significance for the Giver. Of giving up and receiving."

"The horse ran with the train to say goodbye to us."

"Yes. The Giver runs after us when we leave The Highlands, too. It is difficult for the Giver to be separated from you in this way, no matter how necessary it may be. Like Brother. He comes with you—you can feel that, can you not?—and it is intimate and magical. He will come inside you soon. But it is always sad for him to leave you at the train stop, because it is so different for you.

"The horse is wild—but that form is the most domesticated you will ever see the Giver. For the most part, Brother is the tame side of the Giver."

"Yeah, I get it. The coyotes, the bears. . . . So they like to meet their food before they eat it?"

Aubrey laughed.

Harrison presented his next question, although he found he didn't care what the reply would be. "Are the Copies going to try to kill me?"

Aubrey pursed his lips. "I have not seen the orders from the Unseen for your life, so I do not think so. If there were, Brother would have them recalled anyway."

He frowned and glanced at Maggie, which distressed Harrison. Aubrey met his eyes again. "You will have to face them still. But you are prepared for that."

Harrison nodded. "I have my knife."

"No, Harrison," he said urgently. "The knife is not for Copies. You," Aubrey enunciated with a finger in his chest, "do not fight with weapons like we do." He continued to poke him. "You are the secret weapon. You are the magic, the treasure, the quest. You are what they are after, and so you must use the power that is you."

"Me? I'm the weapon? What's this knife in my pocket for then?"

"I think it was to remind you of something." Aubrey's attention again flickered to Maggie.

That's right. He was supposed to talk to her.

Maggie had climbed a ladder to a compact loft area with seating near the glass ceiling of the car. Harrison followed, needing to duck his head at the top, and sat comfortably across from her. They were surrounded by rose and orange sky.

"Maggie. Would you talk to me about how you got this knife?"

She turned from the window and narrowed her eyes at him.

"I thought you didn't want to hear it."

"Well, I know. But I changed my mind." When she didn't respond, he added, "Are you going to pout the whole way home?"

"I can if I want to."

THE HIGHLANDS TUNNEL

Her hostility didn't discourage him. Maggie wasn't one to hold onto resentment, and Harrison knew it. It was time that he apologized.

"Maggie, I'm sorry about the way I treated you. Really, very sorry. If you tell me your story, I promise to believe you."

His softened approach nurtured her trust.

"All right. I'll tell you. But you must believe me. Swear it."

"Yes," he promised.

She swallowed and waited for his nod to begin.

"Yesterday was Sunday, and my aunt was having a fiesta at our house. That's why I'm wearing the special skirt my *abuelita* sent me from Mexico. Anyway, my Tia Serena ordered some special pastries from the bakery for the children and she asked me to go pick up the package."

"Did you walk?" Harrison interrupted. It was not far, but neither was it an easy walk, especially if she would be carrying a parcel back.

"Yes, and I took my time wandering around, since my cousins wouldn't be arriving until later. There were people everywhere in the street."

Harrison watched, mystified, as her mind rewound to the hour of the downtown art fair. She was remembering, not inventing.

"I got a lemonade from the Mighty Midget and was drinking it, when I noticed some men who looked like me. I mean, they were Hispanic, and not family. One man from the group came up to me and complimented my skirt—in Español. He looked . . . strange, but he was definitely Mexican. I could tell when he talked. The dialect was the same as my family's, so I knew he was from our village.

"His eyes were light brown, like caramel, and his hair was very curly, so that it stuck up. Almost like he was *negro*, but his hair color matched the color of his skin, which matched the color of his eyes. Like he was all tan and golden. Very nice looking." She blushed, since she hadn't meant to add that last bit.

Harrison recognized this man as the angry Jamaican who had accused Maggie and chased them. Hearing Maggie's description of the man, he was annoyed with himself for having not been wise to the fake island act. The accent had obviously been exaggerated, and she was right that the coloring hadn't matched at all.

"I turned away from him," Maggie continued, "because I thought he was trying to be rude. But he kept talking to me, and I didn't walk away. I figured it was safe since so many people were around."

"What did he say to you?"

"He said he knew my father. That he was an old friend. That he was in town showing his art, and that he would visit my home before he left. He was telling me things about my father's family in Mexico, and I trusted him."

She looked down, ashamed.

"Did he tell you his name?"

"His name was Delgado."

"Then what?"

"He said he wanted to give me a gift, and he handed me a paper bag." Maggie couldn't resist a present, and even knowing now what was inside those cursed wrappings, her eyes lit up with the retelling. "He told me to open it and then he invited me to come to his booth . . . so we could pick out a gift to give to my father.

"So when he left me, I opened it, and it was the knife."

She gulped.

"Later I found his tent and started looking at the stuff, but I hadn't noticed him yet before I bumped into you."

"You didn't hear him haggling with customers? He was really loud."

"Well, yes, I heard that, but I didn't think it was him, because he was Mexican. And it was so crammed with people. It's a wonder that he saw me! But I think he was careful to look out for me—although I haven't the slightest idea. . . ." She trailed off to pause for a moment. "So anyway . . . the knife on the table caught my eye, because it looked just like the one in my pocket."

Harrison interpreted the rest. "And we were talking and didn't see that he had come to the table and swiped the look-alike knife so he could say you'd shoplifted the one in your pocket."

"You believe me!" she nearly shouted.

"I told you I would. But why didn't you say something when he accused you?"

"I guess I was so shocked by his performance. I wasn't sure if he was being serious or not. Nobody has ever tricked me like that before."

"And you don't know why he would have set you up?"

"No. . . . I keep wondering."

He thought for a while. "You told me in the tent that your father's family is wealthy, and that he made his own fortune as a boxer in Mexico."

"I thought you didn't believe any of that either."

"I think I do now. Then, on the ride here, you said that your father had to get you out of his country because bad people would try to take you."

"Yes, to get money from my father's family."

"Well, do you think this may be about that?"

"Maybe . . . yeah, I guess it's possible. So you really think there could be bad people in Grant?"

"Oh, I think so," he said emphatically. "Let's just hope we're smart enough now to recognize them."

"Right. My *abuelita* always says, "*De noche, todos los gatos son pardos.*"

"Which means. . . ?"

"By night, all cats are gray."

"Which means. . . ?" he asked again.

"I think it means that in the dark, everything looks the same."

"Well, I think we're up against something far worse than cats."

"*Aye yai yai,*" she muttered. "I think we ought to pray for daylight."

THE HIGHLANDS TUNNEL

32. KITE FLYING

After his chat with Maggie, Harrison stood on the platform outside their coach watching The Highlands flash by. In the western distance, the evening sun highlighted the peaks of a snow-crusted granite mountain, causing the dark depressions to run in vertical lines to the horizon. He knew that on the other side of the train he would find the bluish mountain range, like the hills at home. The tracks would lead them that way to the Crossing.

Securing himself to the train, he grabbed onto a pole that stretched from the platform floor to the overhead eaves. Then he leaned out over the speeding ground. The rush was exhilarating.

It was like kite flying. His feet stayed grounded, but something wild and reckless and tethered to him pulled at his arm, urging him to join it. It was the Giver. At first, he had thought it was the other way around: he was the kite and the Giver was the anchor. But now he knew that the Giver was the kite, and all he had to do was let go and he would fly.

Then he heard Aubrey's voice behind him.

THE HIGHLANDS TUNNEL

"I cannot go all the way with you, Harrison."

"I know." That was really too bad.

"The tracks are starting to turn. We will go through the eastern mountain soon, which means—"

"The tunnel is coming," Harrison guessed.

"You ought to come inside now."

Harrison grinned up at the large dark man. "Whatever you say."

"After you," Aubrey said, formally holding the door for the boy. "Aye, you do look ready," he remarked with satisfaction after regarding him for a moment.

"It's been real, Chief," Harrison told him.

Without another word, the big man pulled him into a wholehearted, tingly embrace. Again Harrison was surprised by the sensation, having expected something similar to squeezing a stone monument. Hugging a Laoch was like being dipped in warm chocolate and then licked clean.

Inside the car, the mood was pensive. Wheeler, Juda, and Harry had returned from the dining car. Everyone sat quietly, waiting for the tunnel. The Laochs posed, practicing that statue-still impression they used when they were focused.

Harry came and grasped Harrison's shoulder, smiling at him. Harrison smiled back, but his young grandfather walked past and left him alone.

He used the stillness to center. Brother was keeping his promise. Harrison felt his company. He heard his words, not only falling around him, but covering him, protecting him, burning into his memory.

He was reminded of what was important: Wheeler and Maggie and their folks at home. Most of all, he felt a regard for himself that was unfamiliar but welcome.

He could live in The Highlands and still be present in the Practice World. That was because The Highlands was his home now. He might leave home, but it remained with him. It was his center—his life source—and he didn't think it was ever possible to ride away from that.

No, this wasn't goodbye. He would be back. In fact, he would never really leave.

And then the train entered the tunnel.

There was that same flashing of light on the outside, while everything in between was black, as well as the sense of rapid transport that had more to do with travel in terms of time and realms rather than actual mileage.

Harrison's body shook with the passage, and he closed his eyes, reveling in the experience.

But then it all shut down. The train shuddered to an unhappy halt. The interior lights of the coach flickered on, and Harrison was surprised to find the windows blackened—he could see nothing outside at all. Looking around, he, Maggie, and Wheeler discovered that Harry and the Laochs had disappeared.

THE HIGHLANDS TUNNEL

33. THE TUNNEL REPRISE

"We're still in the tunnel," Wheeler said, scooting close to the other two in the aisle.

Harrison leaned his head to the glass, using his arm to block out the glare from the interior lanterns. He thought he could make out a rock wall.

"Yeah, we're stuck," he groaned.

"I'm going out there," Wheeler announced.

"No!" Harrison and Maggie both shouted at once. They looked at each other for a second, surprised by their simultaneous objection.

"Sit," Harrison ordered his brother, pointing to a seat and watching to make sure he obliged.

"Now what?" Maggie asked Harrison.

"I don't know," he answered truthfully.

She stomped her foot, and the two boys regarded her warily. Then she spun around in frustration, curled up her lip, and clenched her fists at her sides.

"Those great, big, unreliable supernatural beings!" she hissed. "They put us on this train—which supposedly doesn't stop where it's not supposed to, by the way—and sent us through the tunnel, while they just

THE HIGHLANDS TUNNEL

disappear and go on with their previously scheduled existence, which probably has something to do with another party that they didn't want to miss out on with some really rockin' tunes. And I think they forgot to service this thing, or it ran out of coal, or something. Because as soon as they leave, it breaks down. In. The. Dark. Stupid magic train! Stupid mythical creatures!"

She concluded with a shriek that began low in the back of her throat before it came skittering out shrilly from between her teeth. The performance ended with a dramatic collapse into one of the plush velvet seats.

Harrison hesitantly sat next to her. He understood that she had reached her limits and needed to vent. Still he gave her plenty of space, just in case she wanted to hit something.

"Stop looking at me like I'm about to scratch you," she snapped.

"Okay." He quickly looked down at the seat because he wasn't sure he could look her in the eye any other way.

"Maggie," he tried. "It's going to be fine. You're right, the train doesn't make unscheduled stops. We have to trust that this is where it's supposed to be right now. We may be in a tunnel, but that doesn't mean we're stuck. All tunnels have openings. And there's only one way to go, and that's straight forward."

"I don't want to go wandering around in the tunnel. Can't you go check the engine? Maybe you can find the go button."

"That's actually not a bad idea. Wheeler? You

wanna go with me to the engine room?"

No answer.

He yelled again. "Wheel—"

"He didn't!" Maggie growled.

"Oh, no. I think he did." Harrison almost uttered a curse word, but he thought better of it and groaned instead.

As it turned out, Wheeler was not inside the car. Typical Wheeler.

"I've got to go after him," Harrison said. "You stay here."

"I'm not staying here," Maggie argued.

"Please, Maggie. Just let me look out there and make sure it's safe."

"I think we should stay together. That's what's safe."

She was right. The last time he'd tried to leave her, a winged beast from hell had tried to knock her out.

"And when I find Wheeler," she warned, "I'm going to kill him."

"Fine. But let's make sure he's okay before you kill him." Hopefully, for Wheeler's sake, Harrison would find his brother before Maggie did. She looked pretty serious about following through with her threat.

In truth, he was fearful—but not because he thought Maggie would actually kill Wheeler. It was the tunnel and all that it suggested.

One way to get out.

Was this the moment he was supposed to save Maggie? And what about Wheeler out there alone?

THE HIGHLANDS TUNNEL

That greatly compromised his focus. If this tunnel was a time-travel mechanism, might Wheeler have stepped out to another point in time? What was Harrison going to discover out there in the dark?

He took a moment to resolve to be in this story and not make up a new one—like Brother had advised. When he was composed again, he nodded to Maggie and walked toward the front exit.

"Come on then."

They stepped into the vestibule area between their coach and the one in front. With the open stairwell ahead, the energy of the tunnel flowed into the small space. It was coal black—despite the muted light glowing from the train windows, which the tunnel walls absorbed—and they were blind.

Harrison felt his hand along the wall until he found the opening and his foot discerned the first step down. He reached back for Maggie's hand and guided her down behind him.

It was silent. Like the portentous quiet before water boils and the kettle screams.

And then came the ghastly sensation . . . that some*thing* was out there with them in the dark. Its presence was sensed—but not seen with their eyes . . . and it wasn't flesh and blood.

Dread began to rise in Harrison's chest, and then, although his heart continued to batter his insides, he felt numb.

Right before his eyes, out of nothing, a woman materialized. She was elegant and floaty, and she shone.

There was no light in the tunnel but her. She smirked at Harrison, and he felt embarrassed but he couldn't look away.

He heard Maggie's breathing turn quick and erratic. In his dazed state, he wondered flippantly if Maggie could see the beautiful woman, but then he realized she couldn't. If she could see at all in the tunnel, she was seeing something else, because he perceived her head swinging back and forth, vision reaching out into the black to find whatever had joined them.

An angel, Harrison labeled her initially. But then he reckoned that an angel wouldn't look so sardonic. And although she was acting coy, he could tell by the way she studied him that she was fascinated by him. In fact, she was in awe of him.

"Let go of her hand and take mine, Harrison," she breathed, her voice the loveliest sound—similar to when the pretty, popular girl at school acknowledged him.

Holy mother. She knows my name!

"I'll show you the way out." She offered a shimmering, pale, delicate hand.

"Don't trust it."

Out of nowhere, Harrison heard Brother's disembodied voice. As if he were standing right there, it echoed through the tunnel, and he turned to the side expecting to see the Rider. Then he realized that, although Brother may well have been standing undetected in the impenetrable blackness, most likely the voice was in Harrison's head. Neither Maggie nor the ghostly woman reacted to it.

His face must have displayed the instant wariness he felt for the seductress when he heard Brother speak, because the woman looked defensive.

"Follow me. I know the path through. It's this way." The woman floated past Harrison a ways. But she was headed in the wrong direction—back from where they had come.

Harrison's mind reasoned that The Highlands was back that way—didn't he want to go to The Highlands? Wasn't that where he was headed? A cold breeze blew from that direction to encourage his conclusion. But its iciness affected him uncomfortably, in a way that it hadn't when he'd spent all winter day there.

Brother spoke again. **"I'm here,"** he promised. Brother was there in the tunnel, even if Maggie and Harrison couldn't see him.

I would appreciate it if you would stop being so monosyllabic and give me some direction, Harrison thought at Brother. He felt rather than heard his invisible companion's laughter.

"Do you know where Wheeler is?" Harrison asked aloud. The question was for either the voice that sounded like Brother or the specter, he didn't care which. It was the woman who answered.

"Your brother's not in the tunnel, but I'll lead you to him. It's this way."

But she was trying to get him to go backward, and she wanted him to give her the hand that he used to hold on to Maggie. Harrison was unwilling to do either of those things. He shook his head, pleading with his anesthetized senses to wake up.

"I'm sorry," Harrison told her, surprised at the assurance in his own voice, "we're going the other way." He was still deprived of feeling.

"You're wrong," she said, and she lunged suddenly at Harrison. Or he assumed she was coming for him and he tried to duck.

But it flew past him to get Maggie.

"No! You can't have her," he growled and threw himself in its way. He shut his eyes tight and gritted his teeth, expecting to be struck. But when he opened his eyes, the thing had vanished.

His eyes had fortunately adjusted to the dark, and he looked back at Maggie, who had turned exceptionally pale in the murkiness of the tunnel.

"It's all right. We're going forward," he soothed. He used one hand to feel alongside the exterior of the train and the other to pull a trembling Maggie along.

This spooky encounter reminded Harrison again of his dream, and he started to speculate. He couldn't remember what it was that he'd thought to be running from. Although at the end of the dream, he had finally seen it, and it was running away from him. But he couldn't remember *what* it was. Usually the end of the dream was what the mind retained, but he tried and tried and could not recall.

Was this manifestation in the tunnel the Unseen? Was it the Enemy that hated him? This woman had struggled to maintain an elevated smugness, but its attraction—and even trepidation—for Harrison was conspicuous. It was as though Harrison possessed an innate knowledge of this being: manipulative, fiendish, and beautiful . . . but it had no power over him. He knew it and she knew it.

"Wheeler!" Maggie called.

Harrison joined her, shouting his brother's name, but their voices bounced off the walls and seemed to come from every which way. If Wheeler answered, it might take a couple of minutes for the sound to reach their ears.

When they made it to the engine, they noticed light reflecting off its shiny structure. The gleam was not from its headlight as expected but from the tunnel opening in the far reaches.

And then came a welcome sound from the ceiling of the tunnel.

"Look at that!" Wheeler crowed happily.

At once Maggie and Harrison looked up and saw Wheeler sitting astride the top of the engine, between the bell and the smokestack.

Harrison's irritation with Wheeler had morphed into fear when he first stepped out of the train; the fear melded into solace now that he was seeing his little brother again.

Wheeler was pointing at the track ahead, on which was a bright blue and green peacock, prettily making its way toward them from the entrance of the tunnel. Only . . . it was too graceful to be an actual peacock, without that clumsy chicken-like stride had by real-life peacocks.

"I thought only bats lived in caves." Wheeler neatly slid down the round barrel of the engine. He started toward the peacock.

Harrison's natural aversion to birds was kicking in, and Maggie felt a strange sort of foreboding about it, too . . . although it was exquisite. They followed the younger boy for a few steps, keeping their distance.

When Wheeler and the peacock met toe to toe, its tail feathers swept up dramatically into a multi-hued fan, which incredibly blocked all the light from outside the tunnel. It made a stunning blockade in the beam from the train's headlight, and Wheeler stood looking up at the feathers that created a curtain from track to ceiling. The tapestry-like pattern lining its plumes was eerie, making it look like more than one creature. Hundreds of unblinking eyes. . . .

"Get away from it, Wheeler," Harrison commanded.

"Why?" the boy hollered, not bothering to look back over his shoulder.

"It's not a peacock and it's not friendly."

Wheeler began backing up reluctantly.

Behind them, the train rumbled its start-up noises and began to chug forward bit by bit. Soon it seemed that the whole tunnel was shaking with its vibrations, and the bell was clanging incessantly. Meanwhile the kids remained trapped between the bird and the train.

"Run," Harrison told Maggie, pointing in the direction of the opening. He kept hold of her hand, but he

THE HIGHLANDS TUNNEL

wasn't sure what to do about the feathery barricade up ahead. His first objective was to get to Wheeler.

The problem resolved itself a moment later. The peacock folded up, flapped its wings, and levitated in the air of the tunnel, where it transformed to its other form—the wispy, glowing woman Harrison was acquainted with—only she appeared much more sinister. This time, though, his companions saw her, too, and gasped in unison.

Harrison believed himself more capable to deal with the banshee rather than the bird. He plowed into Wheeler, repeating his charge to run. Its eyes narrowed at Maggie as the train picked up speed.

Inspired by his dream, Harrison led his brother in a joint launch against the Unseen (as he was certain now he had *seen* the Enemy in two of its disguises). He seemed to know that it wouldn't hurt him or Wheeler . . . but it wanted Maggie. She ran behind the two boys.

For an absurd moment, Harrison entertained the idea of Brother and the Giver conferring over this plot. *Let's go ahead and add another chase scene to the schedule. . . .*

Either threatened by the brothers or the hurtling train, the Unseen scowled and evaporated. Now the train itself was the immediate danger, so the three kids sprinted to the end of the tunnel, diving into the ditch at the second the train came galloping out.

"Jump on," yelled Harrison, encouraging his companions to get up and get going.

Running after the train again. This was all right

and familiar. Harrison knew they could do this.

He pushed Maggie toward an opening. She missed the first, but managed to grab the banister on the next car. The two boys sprinted beside it. Wheeler hopped up next, followed by Harrison. They stood in the little stairwell catching their breath.

"Alllll Aaaa-board!" Wheeler trumpeted to the sky.

Behind them, reverberating in the tunnel, was heard a disturbing, ghostly laugh.

THE HIGHLANDS TUNNEL

34. WELL-DELIVERED LINES

"What did you think you were doing?" Harrison snarled at his brother. "We told you to stay put."

"Well—I—you—well...." Wheeler stammered. This was just like being in trouble with his mother. He struggled for an explanation but finally determined to try to make Harrison understand. He knew his brother craved an adventure as much as he. "Maggie was throwing a tantrum, and you guys just seemed to want to whine about being stuck. Meanwhile, there was the tunnel out there. And it was so cool! I just couldn't stay still."

Yes, of course; Wheeler was happiest when his heart rate was accelerated.

"Your brother and I talked about it, and we decided that we're going to have to tie you up for the remainder of the trip," Maggie said, looking very stern with her hands on her hips.

"What?"

"Right. Well, we forgot to figure out what we could use to restrain him," Harrison reminded her, playing along.

THE HIGHLANDS TUNNEL

Maggie looked around and noticed Wheeler's perpetually untied Converse sneakers. "We can use his shoelaces."

"Perfect," Harrison commended.

"Nuh-uh. You're not tying me up." Wheeler attempted to call their bluff, but he backed up all the same. This resulted in a short chase down the aisle and over—as well as under—the seats.

The scuffle ended when Harrison caught Wheeler around his ankles, pulling him to the floor. He wanted to smack him over the head but revised instead with a vigorous hair rubbing. The tackle helped to lighten the mood after the disturbance in the tunnel.

It gradually dawned on the train's passengers that time had either rewound or sped up, as it was still daylight on this side of the tunnel. It would be past dark by now in The Highlands. They all wondered where in time they had traveled but hoped it would be somewhere near when their history in the Practice World had left off. Harrison was eagerly wishing it would be back before all the mess had happened; that would be better than to have been missing for a whole twenty-four hours. He wondered if they should get a cover story straight before they arrived, but he wasn't at all sure what they should say.

They talked instead about what would happen when the train stopped in the Crossing.

"Will those awful people be there again?" Maggie asked.

"I sort of think so," Harrison answered truthfully.

"But they're my problem. I want you two to hurry down the alley to the diner as quick as you can. I'll deal with Curtis and Dot."

"Are you sure, bro? If this comes down to a fight, I want to be with you. I'll help you take out Mrs. Byrne," Wheeler offered.

Harrison jerked his head to the side. "I need to talk to you alone for a sec."

Maggie sighed heavily, then turned to face the front of the car. Wheeler walked to the back with Harrison.

"I need you to stay with Maggie."

"Why?"

"She needs protection. I can't let her near those Copies because I think they're going to try to kill her." Wheeler's eyes widened. "Look. Here." Harrison fetched the knife from his sweater pocket and passed it into Wheeler's twitching hand. "Take this, use it if you have to, and keep her safe for me until I can get back."

Wheeler nodded solemnly. "Okay, I will." He stowed the knife in his jeans and walked back to sit with Maggie.

Harrison thought it was appropriate to make a request here. If he was hearing Brother's voice and feeling him when he wasn't physically there, perhaps Brother could hear him, too. If that were the case, Harrison felt it fair to ask him for something. He didn't speak aloud.

Please, Brother, don't let Wheeler have to use that knife.

His silent supplication made him feel better. He

couldn't be sure if it was acknowledged or not, but just for the possibility that it may have been heard, he felt some peace.

The train was slowing, nearing the station. It let out its blasted whistle, alerting whatever horrible monsters were waiting of their arrival.

"I don't want to leave you at the station either, Harrison," Maggie was saying.

"I'll be right behind you. Trust me, I don't want to be away from you either," he said, being straightforward with her.

"But if those vultures are there—"

"Then I'll take care of 'em. You don't worry about it."

"I will worry about it if you're alone with them." She wasn't actually arguing. Maggie felt heartsick at the thought of Harrison confronting the Copies by himself.

"How are we supposed to get down the alley anyway? Won't they be watching for us?" Wheeler asked.

Harrison thought for a moment. "I'll go out first and make a distraction for you. You sneak off and get back home." As he said it, though, he wasn't entirely sure that the Practice World was the safest place. But it had to be better than the Crossing. It was too supernatural there—out of his control.

Before they could protest, he walked to the door and stepped out into the vestibule. He stood in the stairwell and watched the planks of the platform roll into view. When it stopped and the train let out a hiss of steam, Harrison jumped down and waited for the inevitable confrontation.

He didn't have to wait long before he heard the door to the station house slam. It was swinging open on its hinges, hitting the wall repeatedly. He walked to the building. Inside, reclined on one of the benches, was the playacting train engineer.

"Hey there, boy." Curtis greeted him with a smug smile. He held his mouth like he had chewing tobacco in his jaw.

Harrison studied the Copy. *His* Copy. He looked for anything in the face that resembled himself but couldn't find any comparison.

"Hi," Harrison returned, feeling ridiculously casual. He looked around the dark signal house but didn't see Dot.

"How was your trip?" Curtis asked.

"We had some engine trouble in the tunnel, but other than that, it was good. Thanks for asking. Once again the birdlife was particularly . . . sociable."

Curtis chuckled. "Well, glad you could make it back." He stretched his legs out.

"You lied to us," Harrison challenged.

"Now that depends. How do you know it wasn't the other way around? Did you have fun at your little play party?"

"What do you want?"

"Same thing we wanted before you left here last time. We want to keep you here."

"Where's Mrs. Byrne?" he asked. Harrison wasn't

sure how much Curtis knew about what he knew, so he figured he would give the Copy a couple of hints.

"She's watching."

"Is she your supervisor then? I know she outranks you."

Curtis looked ruffled for a moment. Then he smiled again.

"What did she tell you to do to me?" Harrison inquired.

"She can tell you that herself, boy. Why don't you ask her when she gets here?"

"I think I will. I would like to see her now."

"Well, I can't order her around. Like you said, she outranks me. Don't let that scare you, though." He scrunched up his nose with sarcasm.

"I'm not scared. Of you or her." He watched Curtis's face carefully. "Does that scare you?"

He blinked. "No. But I think you should be careful."

"Hmmm. She doesn't outrank *me*. No, I think *you* should be careful," he argued.

"If this newfound confidence comes from the Ransom, I think you ought to know something right now. We won. We killed him."

"From what I understand, the war is not over. You killed him, but he's not gone. You haven't won yet."

Just then, Mrs. Byrne—or Dot rather—entered the room via the ticket booth.

"Mr. Bentley."

"Mrs. Byrne." He was again impressed by her absolutely unremarkable appearance. She was almost a blur.

She looked pointedly at Curts. "The other two are headed to the opening. It's time for you to go."

"No, wait!" Harrison shouted. But Curtis nodded at his superior and disintegrated right there on the bench where he sat.

Harrison started to worry. He assumed he could preoccupy both and didn't anticipate one of the Copies following the others into the Practice World. He would have to make this short.

"Mr. Bentley," Dot spoke again, "go ahead and get comfortable. You will be staying here for a while."

"I don't think I will. . ." then he added as a taunt, "ma'am." It felt so good to defy her that he almost forgot about the danger here. He had never been defiant before. Perhaps passively rebellious and openly mischievous, but never blatantly disrespectful.

"Sit down," she ordered.

"No."

She looked scornfully at him. "Shall I give you work to do? I'm sure we can come up with something to keep you busy. Railroads require a lot of work, you know."

Harrison shook his head. "I don't work for you."

"Then I'll have to bind you."

Her threat reminded Harrison of when Maggie teased Wheeler on the train. Then he had an idea. Maggie's had been an idle remark. Perhaps Mrs. Byrne was bluffing, too.

"You can't touch me, can you?" he asked, suddenly curious.

Dot came toward him, and before he knew what she was doing, she slapped him across the face with such force that he staggered into a bench, which effectively seated him.

"I've been wanting to do that since early September," she said, strangely without feeling. It didn't look like the smack had satisfied her at all.

Harrison held the side of his stinging face in shock. Of course, he should have known. He still wore a scar along his cheekbone from the bird's talon. She had hit him on the other side. They could touch him; they could hurt him. They could *kill* him. Aubrey had warned him about that.

"You always had such a smart mouth. You think I didn't notice your seemingly polite answers in class? You think I don't know you well enough to be able to tell when you're being disingenuous with me? Sarcastic, insolent boy.

"I heard you complaining about me to your schoolmates and family. And getting you to turn in any homework or lab exercises that were worth any credit was like twisting an arm." She grabbed his arm below the elbow and started to slowly turn it. "You would rather be off wasting your time—being boyish and carefree. Well, that's not how reality works, young man."

Harrison didn't want her to recognize the fear he felt or to see the pain from his arm register on his face. "Wow, you've been talking to my mother," he commented dryly.

She got in his face. "You see, Harrison, I know you. I know you as well as I know Curtis. He's part of you, you know. You helped create him—your own personal Copy. And I own him. He must do as I say."

She was talking a lot, but Harrison felt okay about that for the moment. If she tied him up—and he felt pretty sure she could overpower him—that would be it. He was trying to recall all he had recently experienced and determine a solution from what he had learned.

"I don't have to do what you say. My Copy might, but I don't. I'm warning you. Don't touch me!"

"Or what?" she mocked.

"Or else," he cautioned lamely. He closed his eyes and swallowed loudly in consternation at his loss for words. The Copy sneered.

He thought back to that thing in the tunnel. He felt certain it wasn't Dot. She was plain and distracting. That thing was dangerously decorative and frightening. But he had stopped it, hadn't he? He told it no, and it was forced to change course. He had charged the peacock, and it had disappeared.

It was all so frustrating. How was he supposed to fight an enemy that was invisible? A foe that could vanish before your eyes, take on new forms. It could hurt him, but how could he hurt it?

Harrison tried to feel something. He was reaching out beyond himself to find Brother or at least some opportune advice. But he sensed nothing. He was alone. This was one of those times Brother had warned him about—when he would feel abandoned and he would have to believe.

What did he believe?

He decided to speak his beliefs audibly. Some of it he had seen, some of it he had heard, some of it he had perceived. But the words seemed to come from someone else as they left his mouth with unusual evenness of temper.

"I am the Giver's. I belong to the Giver. I am under the Giver's protection. I am the brother of the Ransom, who bears my name across his heart, because he offered his life for mine. I serve them."

She appeared to be taken aback by his words. Halted. She dropped his arm immediately.

In addition to her reaction, Harrison noticed two things occur when he stated his beliefs. First, he realized that it was easy to believe in the supernatural: the Giver and Brother and Laochs and all of that. But it was the belief in who he was in respect to the magic realm that took a leap of faith. As he said it, however, an amazing thing resulted—he believed!

The second thing that happened was such a relief. Brother was with him again. He probably had never left, but for whatever reason, Harrison could feel him again and closer than ever. He knew his words were Brother's words.

"And what makes you think they want you?" Dot hissed. "They have each other and their minions. Why would the immortal have any use for a weak mortal?"

She sort of circled him, keeping some distance between them.

"But I want you, Harrison. There is so much we can do together."

He kept talking as if she hadn't spoken.

"And since I belong to the Giver, I do not belong to you. I will not do as you say anymore."

He remembered Aubrey's declaration: "*You are the secret weapon. You are the magic, the treasure, the quest. You are what they are after, and so you must use the power that is you.*"

"The Ransom is here. You understand what that means for you, right? You lose. You can do nothing."

Then Harrison turned rather bold, standing up. He glared at her through hooded eyes, and he actually *saw* her for the first time. But she was not a she at all—no longer Dot in her bland, brown disguise—but a gruesome, wrinkly fiend. So small and furious. He was no longer afraid, and he heard Brother whisper his name, his true name, in the Highland language.

Never. It was all the inspiration he needed, and he shouted it out loud.

"YOU WILL NEVER TOUCH ME AGAIN!"

The Copy wailed and was thrown back into a bench and restrained by a sort of invisible shackle. It gnashed and struggled and howled curses in some otherworldly tongue.

Harrison looked at it and was not repulsed or afraid. Rather he found its pitiful outburst amusing, and he wanted nothing more than to laugh. He twisted his mouth instead to hide his smile and did the most powerful thing he could think to do. He turned around and walked away.

And although he doubted the truth of his farewell statement, he couldn't help but throw out one last smart remark.

"See you in class, Mrs. Byrne."

35. Muy Peligroso

Harrison didn't remain to watch his former physics teacher take on any new forms. He wasn't definite that she would stay bound, so he figured it best to hurry on to the diner's back door.

Besides, there was that other lowlife Curtis to worry about.

As he walked away from the train station and crossed the road to head up the alley, he noted the hazy glow of the streetlamps. The sky, too, was the same twilight gray as when he had crossed here before.

Coming to the back side of the little metal kitchen, he wondered if he would find another confrontation inside. But the interior was dreadfully quiet, and the order window was closed. Despite its physically limiting size, the diner felt as dark and vast as a cathedral—too hallowed for anything wicked to muck about here. Outside, however, he could hear the animated goings-on of the art festival.

Harrison felt dissected in a way, like he had left parts of himself in The Highlands. It was disorienting to hear a crowd of normal people on the other side of the dividing wall. The environment was confusing to Harrison, who was not yet whole, and he painstakingly thought it out.

Yesterday—the day the trouble started—was Sunday. He had spent one night in The Highlands. Today would be Monday then. The artists and wares should be packed up and gone, and Main Street would be closing up for the weekday evening onset.

Harrison blew out a big breath. The train must have carried them back a day, to the time when they had traveled out of the Practice World. Now he was back, and it was as if no time had passed at all.

This solved the problem of their long absence, but it also created a new problem. Or rather it re-presented the original debacle: some lunatic wanted to harm Maggie.

Once the realization sank in, the urgency of the situation caught up to Harrison, and he practically flew out the side door and into the crowded street.

He was a stranger. Like an expatriate come back after decades out of country. How much of himself had he left in the supernatural realm? This sensation was bewildering—physically being in a place but not *really* being there.

It was almost like walking in a dream. Nobody paid him any attention, but he was remarkably aware of each life, each personality, each identity with whom he shared this space. He belonged with them, and yet he was separate from them. Perhaps, he thought, he wasn't the dreamer at all; perhaps he was the only one actually awake.

But he pressed on and gradually came to awareness with the repetition of this mantra: *Maggie and Wheeler are here somewhere. I have to find them.*

No sign of his cohorts.

Down the road he could see his accident being cleaned up. He walked along that way on the far side of the street, crouching between streams of people and keeping his face hidden. He passed the tent with the weapons and tried to casually peek inside.

It was still packed with visitors, and he noticed right away that a different man—definitely Hispanic—was peddling the weaponry; he was much quieter than the previous imposter.

Harrison walked past the booth a few yards then hesitated. He remembered that the man—Delgado, Maggie called him—and the police officer had chased them toward the diner. So he backtracked, looking for any clues that Maggie and Wheeler had been caught.

He thought back to their last minutes hiding out with Harold and recalled the metal plating being beaten on from the outside. If it had been this Delgado or the policeman rattling the Mighty Midget, perhaps Maggie and Wheeler had been caught there. Then where might they be? The police station? Jail?

Or that demented Curtis might have caught up with them. What would he want? What could he do to them? Harrison hadn't heard Mrs. Byrne give any specific orders.

Or . . . Maggie and Wheeler might be safe at home.

THE HIGHLANDS TUNNEL

Of course, that potential outcome sounded too good to even consider with the way their journey had progressed so far.

Come on, Harrison pleaded with Brother again. *You've got to give me some idea! How am I supposed to do this without any guidance? I need a sign. Something. Please?*

As he neared the Mighty Midget Kitchen for the second time, he noticed his and Wheeler's bikes propped up in the bicycle rack on the opposite sidewalk.

Wheeler would have ridden his bike home. He was still here.

As Harrison approached it, the entrance to the diner blew open and a gust of cold wind and snow flew at Harrison's face. He came thoroughly awake with the brisk reminder of winter in The Highlands. No one else on the street seemed to notice the brief ice storm that had come sweeping out of the magic camper during that late spring evening.

He walked back into the Mighty Midget with renewed interest. Ignoring the door that led to the Crossing, he found another exit on the opposite end. He stepped to it and put his ear to the metal. At first it was quiet on the other side . . . but then he heard a faint galloping. The Giver!

He turned the handle immediately, but what he saw caused his stomach to fold.

There was no horse. No Giver.

He *had* found Maggie and Wheeler, thankfully,

some ways away, in the alley that ran between the two buildings behind Harold's kitchen. This was not the Crossing—Harrison recognized right away the brick retaining wall that stood on the other side of the road in the place of the train station. A green van was parked in the fire lane.

The man Delgado held Maggie in his grip and was trying to drag her toward the vehicle. The police officer restrained Wheeler, who looked at Harrison with a mixture of alarm and relief. When Harrison's eyes left Wheeler's and glanced up at the policeman's face, he was met with the now familiar blue beams that belonged to Curtis. His menacing glower said, *Look, the brother got away before, but I got him this time.*

So the Copy was working with the guy who wanted Maggie, Harrison realized. A wave of shame and disgust rolled through his gut when he realized that his Copy was trying to get the girl, too. *Evil*, Brother had called him—*a worthy adversary.*

He should have figured something was going on when the man involved the police. If he indeed intended to take Maggie for a ransom or whatever, why would he fetch the real authorities?

The Mexican-Jamaican didn't notice Harrison because he was too preoccupied trying to keep Maggie in check. She was struggling against his pull with all her might, and Harrison thought that she, too, must have recognized Curtis in this other disguise. That and the fact that they had been dragged into a desolate alley didn't project a happy future.

THE HIGHLANDS TUNNEL

Harrison approached the scene miserably, not knowing what to do. He couldn't sneak up, as there was nowhere to hide, and Curtis was already aware of his presence. When it registered with the Copy that the boy had escaped from his superior, he looked confused and vaguely shocked. Harrison's presence here was not part of the plan apparently.

Wheeler was mouthing something to him, but he had to edge closer to distinguish the words. *The knife*, he was saying.

The knife!

How would he get the knife from Wheeler when Curtis was holding him? Harrison shook his head and shrugged.

Arms held tight behind his back, Wheeler jerked his head at Harrison, in a movement quite like the Giver's horse persona. His eyes pointed significantly at the ground past Harrison. His older brother finally understood, turned around, and searched the broken asphalt and gravel. There. He spied it just beyond the threshold of the metal door. Wheeler must have dropped it coming out of the diner. The answer to his small request that Wheeler not need to use the knife, Harrison supposed.

Curtis, shuffling with Wheeler, half dragging and half kicking him along, was making his way to the van. Probably to stuff Wheeler in it so he could help Delgado wrangle Harrison and Maggie.

Harrison snatched up the knife and ran past Curtis and his brother. After overcoming Dot, he was certain he could conquer this lesser Copy as well. Easy. He must bypass Wheeler, who would serve to keep Curtis's hands busy for the moment so he could save Maggie.

Surprised, she found Harrison's eyes and whispered a heads-up in Spanish. *"Peligro."*

Several times over the course of their adventure he'd overheard Maggie using that word under her breath. She was warning him . . . not that he needed a warning. He knew this fellow wasn't right.

"Muy peligroso," she whispered again before otherwise occupying her mouth. She clamped down hard on the man's leg with her teeth.

"Ah!" Delgado groaned after a theatrical half minute of stomping his feet and twisting his hands.

Harrison ran to where the attacker and victim—not sure who was who at this moment—stood tangled. He told himself begrudgingly—and with some amusement in spite of the trauma—*Like she needs* me *to save her!*

As expected, the attacker released Maggie to hold the wounded part of his leg.

Harrison smartly prowled up behind and pressed the knife to the man's neck. Delgado's squally brass-colored eyes glared at him with agitation and wonder. He searched for Maggie, who wasn't far away.

"Get her!" he yelled in his genuine inflection to Curtis.

Although Harrison continued to hold the blade to the man's throat, he only meant to threaten him with

THE HIGHLANDS TUNNEL

it. The plan was to bargain with Delgado. He was not an experienced fighter, having participated in nothing more violent than mock wrestling with Wheeler and even his father when he was younger. No one foresaw that Harrison would someday need that particular skill.

But Delgado hadn't grown up in Grant; he'd experienced a very different sort of upbringing, in which fighting was as normal for him as running away was for Maggie.

So he elbowed Harrison in the belly, which caused the boy to double over. Seeing his opportunity to gain the advantage, he tore the knife with minimal effort from Harrison's right hand. They fell together to the road, Delgado on top and Harrison trapped under his trembling body.

The knife moved as if it had a mind of its own, for the enemy did not intend to harm the boy. But it was a knee-jerk reaction to being attacked, and the knife would take his revenge. It plunged in the man's hand, downward over Harrison's chest.

As time decelerated for the end of his story, Harrison watched the blade coming for him, and he told himself, *This is it.* He even heard the galloping horse again. The Giver was on the way. He hoped that the Giver came to save Maggie and Wheeler now that he couldn't.

But also in that much-talked-about slow-motion play of an individual's last seconds of life, he felt a violent push. Before he knew that he was out from under the knife, he saw a body take his place under the man.

It was the Ransom, his eyes glowing and bright green.

Brother, laid out on the ground where Harrison had been, looked the boy right in the eye and grinned his more humble crooked smile. His arms were extended, held out straight in a passive gesture that meant he wouldn't try to fight his murderer.

The knife didn't stop; the attacker didn't register the change of victims. It stuck Brother between his ribs and he gritted his teeth together, absorbing the sharp pain of the stabbing.

This is no ghost, Harrison thought, unwilling to look away from the violence. *He bleeds.*

Curtis looked triumphant. Wickedly gleeful.

Delgado, seeing finally what he had done, gasped. He hadn't even noticed the switch until the blood was spreading from the gash. Locking eyes with Brother then, he changed from vicious bully to fearful penitent. Standing up shakily, he didn't speak but stumbled away, past Curtis and Wheeler to the back entrance of the Mighty Midget Kitchen. He kept looking backward at the accidental slaughter until he was finally swallowed up into the metal diner, from which he would make his escape and continue to flee, forgetting his van.

Brother, who was trying to sit up, let him go with a last pitying glance. Then he turned his attention to the police officer. He narrowed his eyes at him and—strangely—bared his teeth.

Out of the Mighty Midget Kitchen rushed a small

band of Laochs, charging forward with their weapons. Some snarled. Some roared. Some ran ahead and crouched, ready to pounce. They were formidable and fantastic.

Curtis, whose satisfaction swiftly turned to fear, frantically drew in a ragged breath, dropped Wheeler's arms, and then performed his quick vanishing act barely before the Laochs pounced and evaporated with him. He left a clutter of feathers where he had stood.

All three kids clung to Brother. His breathing was irregular and he grunted when he moved. They helped the remaining Laochs—those few who hadn't pursued the Copy—pull him to the wall, which he leaned against, wheezing.

"Help me with this," Brother asked Harrison, sounding very thirsty. Harrison's teeth dug into the side of his cheek as he tugged to remove the stubborn knife from Brother's chest and lay it on his pant leg. "Maggie's burden," Brother whispered reverently. Then he dug the leather sheath from his pocket and covered the bloodied blade.

Maggie was crying against his shoulder. When Harrison noticed Brother's blood clotting in her hair, he took off his sweater and held it to the wound. There was so much blood; he thought he saw it coming from Brother's mouth, too.

"*Gracias, Hermano,*" Maggie whispered in Brother's ear. "Will you be all right?"

"Yes. It will be a scar soon. An important one," he assured her in a scratchy voice, winking at Harrison then cocking his head in his direction. "He fought for you, Maggie."

"*Gra*—thank you, Harry—Harrison," Maggie stuttered, turning to look at her would-be rescuer, her black eyes an aquarium of tears.

Harrison grimaced and pulled back the sweater-bandage to examine the wound, although it made him lightheaded to do so. He was curious, wanting to see if this mark would have his name on it or Maggie's or Wheeler's . . . maybe even Delgado's. When it was visible, he saw that the knife had pierced where the old scar had been—his scar . . . the one that was labeled with his name. Where the name would be was blotched with blood and therefore illegible.

Harrison imagined that the scar he saw before in The Highlands was something of a phantom scar. Or perhaps, he thought, a better description would be *prophetic*. It bore his name. It may have worn other names, too, but it was his mark. It foretold this tragedy.

"It's not a tragedy," Brother said suddenly, reading Harrison's thoughts. "It's a gift."

"We should get help," Wheeler suggested, looking up at Aubrey and Juda, who towered solemnly over their heads.

"Harry will be in the kitchen," Calista replied.

"I'll go with you," Maggie offered, wiping her face with the backs of her hands. She, Calista, and Wheeler jogged off toward the Mighty Midget, Harrison and Brother watching.

"They'll be safe, right?" Harrison asked.

"Yes," Brother promised. "The enemy is gone." Harrison knew he wasn't referring to the human. "This," he said, waving his hand over the injury, "renders the enemy useless."

"What do we need to do for him?" Harrison asked the Laochs, who still carried their weapons.

Brother answered. "I'll be fine. Really." He smiled his assurance. "It hurts now, but I just need to go home. These guys will help."

A pang of nostalgia filled Harrison's chest—so full that it hurt. "Can I go back with you?" he asked. Then he decided he wanted a concrete answer, and he knew Brother was likely to speak in code, so he added a specific. "Tonight?"

The Laochs chuckled tensely.

"No." Brother offered an apologetic smile.

Despite the refusal, Harrison was amazed. *My first real no from him. I guess there is a first time for everything.*

Brother grinned broadly at Harrison's thoughts. "Like the blood, my no is my gift to you."

"Then why did you give me this?" Harrison pointed to the tainted knife.

"Maggie didn't want it, and you happen to be the right man to carry it for her. I suppose I should have given you this with it." Brother reached again into his shirt pocket and lifted out a folded card.

"What's this?" Harrison asked, taking it. A corner was reddened with saturated blood.

"A postcard."

"Thanks."

"You can read it later."

He nodded.

"What of Hector?" Brother asked the Laochs, his eyes fluttering a bit.

"He's with Alejandro," Juda reported. "The amigos went looking for him after he caused the scene on the street. They are going to pack up the booth and take him home. He shouldn't be able to get back in the country."

"Good." Brother nodded.

"Are you talking about Delgado?" Harrison figured.

"Mmm," Brother mumbled. "His friends started to worry when he showed an interest in Maggie. They don't want any trouble. . . . I'll tell you about it later." Brother's breathing was getting worse.

Harold came hurtling out of the diner with Maggie and Wheeler. He was elderly again, wearing his white apron and cap.

"Can he walk?" he asked urgently.

"We can carry him," said an Ancient One.

"Wait," Brother whispered. He was feeble but his hands were startlingly strong as they gripped Harrison's neck and pulled so that the boy's forehead touched his. He used his thumbs to put pressure on either side of Harrison's nose. "You'll need to breathe," he said, releasing the boy. "Okay, I'm ready."

"Let's get you inside," Harold told Brother as the Laochs lifted him to his feet and walked his staggering form carefully to the entrance. Maggie stayed by his side, holding the sweater to the injury.

THE HIGHLANDS TUNNEL

Brother stumbled in the door and folded up on the floor of the Mighty Midget Kitchen.

Somehow all of the Laochs fit inside, too. Harold made a compress with a cloth that he ran under cold tap water. Wheeler pressed it to Brother's head, which was beaded with sweat.

"He's got to get back to The Highlands," Wheeler guessed.

His grandfather confirmed with a nod.

Harrison looked around. "I thought you all weren't scheduled to come back on the train until tomorrow."

"Technically today is yesterday . . . so I suppose we never left," Aubrey answered with a wink.

Brother was becoming weaker.

"So how do we get him back?" Wheeler asked, looking up at the grim Laochs. "How do you get back?" he then asked Brother softly.

"I called for a ride," he murmured, his voice husky and tired.

Maggie held Brother's head and he whispered something to her.

There was a crude banging on the door that led to the Crossing. A Laoch opened it. It was the horse—the Giver had come to pick up its rider.

Its expression was indescribable for the sheer number of passions playing there. The horse's face and posture were a blend of pathos and pride and every feeling necessary to combine the two.

And then Harrison understood: the Giver was Brother's parent. Only a parent would look that rattled.

Brother started to slump.

"I think he's dying," Maggie cried. "Brother . . . don't. No, please."

"Don't worry, Maggie," Harrison consoled. "He said he would be all right. We've got to get him on the horse."

"He's dead!" she screeched. "He's not breathing!" Her eyes swept from the giants to the horse, which stood in the Crossing. "Please, do something. . . ."

The Laochs hoisted Brother's collapsed form, carried him out to the Crossing, and pushed him up on the horse's back.

Calista was speaking to Maggie emphatically in Spanish as they positioned the Ransom on his mount. Maggie nodded and wiped her tears. Then she said gently in English, "Brother will be restored to life. It's just his form that is broken. Do you believe this?"

"Yes," Maggie sniffed.

"Good. Then you will see him again." She smiled and joined the others outside the door.

"We need to catch the train," Harold announced, meaning himself and the Laochs. "This is for your father," he said, handing Wheeler a bag, presumably containing the promised hot dog. Then the old man embraced Maggie and his grandsons and stepped through the portal, transforming into a young pilot before their eyes.

"Go home," Aubrey commanded from the other side. "Do not be afraid. The Enemy did not win today."

THE HIGHLANDS TUNNEL

The Laochs gave a subdued cheer, raising their weapons in a farewell salute.

Harold and the Ancient Ones turned to go down the alley, respectfully waiting to escort their fallen hero.

The horse took a last grateful look at the three of them left in the little capsule. Followed by Harry and its band of soldiers, the Giver trotted away, Brother's limp body absorbing the bounce of the movement. Maggie, Wheeler, and Harrison watched until it rounded the corner and was out of sight.

36. Going Home

As in a trance, Wheeler and Harrison fetched their bikes and walked with Maggie while she picked up the pastries from the bakery for her family's party.

When they reached the fork in the road, Harrison suggested that Wheeler head on home with the hot dog and let their parents know he would be on his way after escorting Maggie. Wheeler suggestively waggled his brows and made a couple of cheeky comments about their needing time alone.

"Vamos!" Maggie ordered, helpfully pointing out the way.

Harrison rolled his eyes as his brother rode off in the direction of their farmhouse, waving and making loud kissing noises. The other two didn't feel so humorous.

"C'mon," he said to Maggie, while strapping the box of pastries to the back of his bicycle. "How about a lift?" He motioned to his handlebars.

She eagerly climbed up after he straddled the bike seat and steadied it for her. He pushed off and they were rolling lazily down the dirt road toward Maggie's father's trailer.

Both were pensive, but content to be in each other's company. The girl's hair slapped Harrison's face, and he smiled when she frowned back at him, sheepishly trying to tether her long locks into a braid. The braiding reminded them of Brother, and a stream of mourning ran its course through their bodies, somehow connected by the bike and the shared experience.

Harrison pitifully sought out Brother's presence in the wind as he traveled, but he couldn't find it.

"Brother said that Delgado's friends made him leave. He won't be back," he said, "but I think, just to be safe, you ought to stay at home for tonight. At least don't go out alone for a while."

Maggie nodded soberly.

All too soon it seemed to Harrison, the bike was crossing the Castillo-Rios property line. Harrison skidded to a stop, and all at once he was nearly blown over by hope.

Something heavy rolled, and light came into the tunnel. A way. . . .

"Did you hear that?" he asked Maggie excitedly.

"The horse?" she confirmed.

They looked around for a rider and mount but saw neither. The galloping came nearer and nearer until it thundered painfully in their heads, when it abruptly cut off. Their ears still thudded with the echo of the sound.

And then Harrison felt Brother again. This time he wasn't beside him or hovering in the air. He was inside of him. It was a gentle invasion, and Harrison was no more an empty body in the Practice World. The Highlands had come to stay inside of him, and Brother was The Highlands. The Ransom's words melded with the thoughts in the boy's mind, and he smiled a welcome back.

He and Maggie euphorically traipsed the rest of the way to her door. They heard the fiesta enduring spiritedly in the backyard—the occasional shriek or laughter rising above the rest. The volume of the music strained against the limits of the speakers, pushing to be free. Harrison thought that Maggie had probably felt quite comfortable during those meadow musical celebrations in The Highlands . . . if this was a normal part of life for her. And he suspected she was a girl who knew how to party.

"Brother wants to tell you something," he ventured.

She nodded enthusiastically. She felt him, too.

" 'I told you I would be all right, *chica*.' "

Maggie laughed.

"And he wants me to give you this . . . but I don't know if I should," Harrison teased, knowing Maggie couldn't resist a present.

"Oh, please!" she begged, and he leaned down and kissed her sweetly on the cheek.

Reaching her fingers to where the kiss was left, she held onto it. Then she closed her eyes and smiled.

"Adios!" she chirped and skipped inside, skirt flouncing in her wake, displaying its hidden colors like a flag in the wind.

He automatically knocked on the door after she'd shut it in his face. She reopened with a quirked eyebrow.

"Um . . . oh, do you think I could borrow some half-and-half . . . or cream . . . or something?"

"Oh, sure. Hold on. Let me look."

She returned a moment later with a small carton of heavy cream.

"I think that will work. Thanks."

"Bye, Harry"—Maggie smiled; it was an intentional mistake—"son, I mean." Then she leapt at him, returning his kiss from earlier. She slammed the door again.

"Be safe," he whispered to it.

He left Maggie to the love and protection of her family, feeling confident that the Giver was here, too, watching out for her.

Trudging back to his bicycle, he was inspired to leave it for Maggie. He decided he would ask his father for a horse instead and see what that would get him. He rolled the bike around to lean against a tree and then checked his pockets for any paper or pencil—some way to let her know it was a gift from him. He felt the card from Brother in his jeans pocket and abandoned the project.

Without hurrying, he made a direct path in the southwest direction, toward home, not bothering to take the road. The sunset played brilliantly to his right. The shadowy woods on his left provided a welcome concept. Like always, he ached to veer off his course and go trekking through the dark trees. Anything could be hiding in those woods. That mystery kept him present in the Practice World.

Unfolding the postcard, he devotionally touched the blood that stained the edge. It pictured the beach in The Highlands, which charmed Harrison. There was a paper folded inside, and he opened it to read what Brother had written.

Harrison~

By now you know that I am inside of you. It's where I live when we are not in The Highlands together. This letter is a reminder of our story. Wasn't it a grand adventure?

Next time I will come to fetch you and there will be other thrills.

With the wound that I took for you this evening, I am presenting you a gift. It is the gift of your heart—a gift worth protecting. Ask any Laoch. Ask your grandfather. They would trade it all for a chance at humanity.

I am that fond of you, my boy—I am giving you your life in exchange for mine. It's finished now, but I would do it again and again for all eternity.

Can you live in a world in which you can't see me walking beside you? Can you live in the world

THE HIGHLANDS TUNNEL

without seeing me at all, but live believing that I am with you? If anyone can do that, I know it's you.

This is my gift to you, Harrison. Live in the world. Create in it. Breathe in it. Get into trouble. Get dirty.

Live.

Remember all the words we shared in The Highlands.

Words are so important, Harrison. You can create anything with your words. When you use my words, the magic is even more powerful . . . as a creative force and, yes, as a weapon.

As long as you listen to my voice, you will always hear me. If you stop listening, or start believing other voices, it will be harder to hear me. And there will be times when you will think I stopped talking to you, or that I abandoned you. But I will never leave you. And I always go with you.

Believe me.

The Giver has given me to you. I am here, and I will give you what you need—even what you want.

Try to see yourself as I see you. I love you.

Your Brother

There was more on the back.

Postscript: Maggie will be fine.
PPS. The knife is not for fighting!

All right. Jeez. Harrison didn't know what had happened to the knife anyway.

He folded the letter and postcard back and tucked the packet in his pocket, keeping a hand wrapped around it. He grinned widely and plodded through the spring pastures to his parents' home, carton of cream swinging by his side.

As he journeyed, he saw the sun set for the very first time and gave himself permission to anticipate the coming darkness.

THE HIGHLANDS TUNNEL

Epilogue

There was a delicate, continuous knocking on the front farmhouse door. Their father had just finished turning the lights on inside after the family had eaten a dinner of asparagus quiche, made with cream instead of half-and-half.

Wheeler looked at Harrison hopefully.

The older brother shook his head. "It's not him. His knock wouldn't sound like that anyway."

"Yeah, you're right." Wheeler sighed. "Maybe it's Harry?"

"I don't think so. . . ."

"Hello, Helen," their father greeted politely, letting the cool evening air into the house.

"Cort. I don't mean to be a bother, and I hope I'm not interrupting your supper," Mrs. Dunbar said with practiced Southern decorum.

"Not at all. We just finished. What can I do for you?" he said, stepping out on the porch with the old lady and pulling the door closed.

Harrison and Wheeler stood by the windows in the front room listening to Mrs. Dunbar tell her story.

"I just want to make sure everything's all right. I was at the artisan fair downtown earlier today and saw your oldest boy running from a police officer." She sucked in a sharp breath. "He was with two other young people. One was that Spanish-speaking girl."

She deftly disguised her desire for gossip with feigned concern. "I didn't know what to do at the time, but I thought I would come over and see if I could help in any way."

Their father took a moment before he spoke.

"Well, I thank you, Helen. But this is the first I've heard about it. The boys rode their bikes into town this evening, but I assure you neither came home in the back of a patrol car . . . not this time anyway. Perhaps it was another boy you saw. Do you need a ride back? It's getting quite dark."

His father's simple distraction and easy gallantry impressed Harrison. It seemed to shut Mrs. Dunbar up and she did accept the ride. He hadn't thought much about the events that had started their adventure since he got home—he was instead focused on Brother, getting used to his company—but he realized that he needed to talk to one of his parents right away. He had damaged property during the chase and wouldn't feel right if he didn't correct it somehow.

His dad came home several minutes later but didn't say anything to Harrison. He moved about the kitchen, helping to clean up. Maybe he was feeling charitable since, thanks to his sons, he hadn't had to fill up completely on quiche but started with a hot dog appetizer.

Harrison was drying dishes with his mother.

"Harrison! You have a scar. When did that happen?" Annie Bentley asked with maternal concern, grazing a hand across his mended cheekbone.

The blood drained from his face when he thought at first Mrs. Byrne had left a mark when she slapped him. His fingers felt their way under his eye, and he remembered the hawk talon had ripped his skin there.

"Um. . . . When I got scratched by that bird. Falconry accident. You know," he pretended.

"What?" Annie looked at her eldest son, incredulous. She hadn't seen this scar before. Wheeler often chased chickens, but she never knew Harrison to go anywhere near a bird since the rooster pecked a hole in his foot those years ago.

Annie's edge wore off when her son flinched. She tenderly brushed the backs of her fingers over the mark. "Scars are very handsome on a man," she said. It was then that her son saw Annie the way he would in The Highlands—in the light of the bonfire. She was a warrior queen—gentle but powerful. Perhaps she saw the man in Harrison, too.

Harrison smiled, in awe of her. And yet, she was still curious. He chose to change the subject to distract his mother from the inevitable interrogation. "Dad, can I talk to you?"

"Of course." He looked expectant and delighted to be asked. "Annie? I'll finish drying when we're done."

"Oh, I'll get them. You two go on," she said kindly.

To his son, Cort suggested they sit on the front

porch.

"Thanks again for the hot dog," he whispered when they were outside.

"No problem," Harrison answered. He was pleased by this new intimacy created by the secret hot dog and the problem he was about to confess. "Uh . . . something happened during our time in town."

"So I heard. Go on."

Harrison looked at his father's face expecting apprehension but saw only interest.

"Well, I ran into Maggie Rios in one of the artists' booths. We talked for a while, and then the vendor came over and accused her of stealing. I was standing right with her the whole time, but he launched into her—"

"I'm sure I can guess why that was," Cort muttered, repelled by their small town's petty prejudices.

"Anyway, she said she didn't take it, and I believed her. The guy called over a police officer, and all I could think to do was run. So we took off."

"That explains Helen Dunbar's appearance tonight," he said dryly. "You didn't get caught?"

"No, not exactly. The whole thing was a mistake. Like I thought, Maggie didn't steal anything. Problem is, during the chase, I knocked over a shelf of merchandise."

His father's concerned blue eyes reminded Harrison of Brother. "Ohhh. That is a problem. What do you want to do?"

"I thought maybe we could go back . . . together.

You know—I just want to make it right." *I want you with me*, he wanted to say.

"Will I need my wallet?" his father asked.

"Oh, yeah. Maybe." Harrison turned shy, digging the billfold out of his back pocket and handing it over without meeting the man's eyes.

With quiet and understanding, Cort Bentley drove his son back to the darkened Main Street. Most of the vendors were still packing up.

As they walked by, Harrison noted that Harold's diner was closed up. It looked to him mysterious, slightly dangerous, and sort of attractive, like an unloaded handgun. A hidden portal to another level right on Main Street. A lot of bad things had happened there, but it was still a sacred place for Harrison, part of his life's geography. An altar of sorts to remember that his experience in The Highlands had really happened.

He also noticed that he expected Brother to show up at any moment. The Rider had become so unpredictable, appearing and disappearing, that Harrison felt constantly prepared for his arrival. Or the arrival of anything, rather. What might be coming, good or bad . . . he expected the unexpected. He was ready to be surprised.

They were relieved to find the artist couple who had been showing their pottery when Harrison collided with it. They were very gracious and even more appreciative when his father wrote a big check to cover the damage.

THE HIGHLANDS TUNNEL

Harrison apologized profusely and explained why he had been running. He felt terrible that he hadn't even helped clean up the mess, but he didn't really have an excuse that he could offer them.

"I'm so sorry, Dad," Harrison said on the ride home, his head hanging.

His father nodded. "What I want to know is . . . what did Wheeler do? Where was Wheeler in all of this?"

Harrison grimaced.

"I know that you cover for him," his father revealed.

"It really was all my fault, Dad. Wheeler just came along for the ride."

His dad looked at him, disbelieving.

"Why aren't you angry at me?" Harrison asked.

Cort surprised him with a smile. "Well, I don't think you ought to run from the police again. But I think you had noble intentions. Let's save angry for when you steal a car or something. Besides, you can earn the money to pay me back."

"Maybe I can get a job at the Mighty Midget," Harrison mused.

"Nonsense. You can work for me."

"Really?" Harrison asked with enthusiasm.

"Sure. This summer. I'll talk to your mother. I need a cheap laborer." Cort smirked.

Harrison was delighted. "I would really like that." Then his face fell. "Oh. But you know if Mom finds out about this trouble, she's going to be mad at you for not grounding me . . . unless, you know . . . you don't tell her," he added hopefully.

His father thought. "Well, I can't not tell her. But I'll say that I busted you for it and that I'm forcing you to complete hard manual labor to pay back your debt. She'll believe that working for me would be punishment enough."

Harrison was smiling again. "You know what the best part will be?" he asked his father. "We can eat hot dogs every day."

His dad chuckled. "My treat," he offered.

"Dad?"

"Yeah?"

"Want to watch *X-Files* with me tonight? It's Sunday."

"You got physics homework?" he checked.

Harrison shook his head. He most definitely did not.

"Well, okay. I didn't know you really liked that show. Don't you think it's too . . . out there?"

The son grinned. "No, not at all," he answered. Harrison was finding that he liked to believe.

THE HIGHLANDS TUNNEL